TRUST ME

Claire Lorrimer

This first world edition published 2015
in Great Britain and the USA by
SEVERN HOUSE PUBLISHERS LTD of
19 Cedar Road, Sutton, Surrey, England, SM2 5DA.
Trade paperback edition first published 2015
in Great Britain and the USA by
SEVERN HOUSE PUBLISHERS LTD.

British Library Cataloguing in Publication Data

Lorrimer, Claire author.
  Trust me.
  1. Triangles (Interpersonal relations)--Fiction.
  2. Vacations--Spain--Fiction.
  I. Title
  823.9'14-dc23

ISBN-13: 978-0-7278-8499-2 (cased)
ISBN-13: 978-1-84751-598-8 (trade paper)
ISBN-13: 978-1-78010-649-6 (e-book)

Typeset by Palimpsest Book Production Ltd.,
Falkirk, Stirlingshire, Scotland.

Printed digitally in the USA.

To Cynthia, whose assistance was invaluable, with gratitude. C.L.

PROLOGUE

I am standing at the top of the black ski run with my wife, Leena. The sky is a brilliant blue, the snow dazzling in the hot sunlight. It is early and there is no one in sight.

Leena is looking at me, impatient for us to start down the run. It has been closed for two days because the unusually heavy frosts have made it too dangerous. But yesterday the sun came out and now they have removed the no-go barriers.

Today I am filled with tension and excitement. Today I am going to kill my wife.

'You go first, Leena; you're faster than I am, but be careful, it will still be very icy. This black ski run is tricky enough even for the expert skiers, so no wonder it's been closed for the past few days.'

My good luck. The weather has given me a chance to do it . . . to get rid of her and get control of all that money she has left me in her will. We start down and Leena is leading. She thinks she is a better skier. She probably is.

No, not this next bend . . . catch her up now or it will be too late . . . nobody following us. Sun is reflecting off her white ski suit . . . God knows what that outfit cost . . . only worn it once and this will be the last time . . . Now! Quickly . . . catch up . . . lean over . . . one shove with my shoulder . . . she's screaming . . . she's gone.

I can't catch my breath . . . didn't see how far she fell . . . I must go back, make sure I pushed hard enough for her to miss the rocks and go down, down into the ravine. Check nobody is coming! Taking my skis off . . . be quicker. Careful now, nearly fell. Stopping to listen . . . she's not calling for help. Look again, must make sure . . .

Wake up! Wake up now before the bad bit – the terrifying minutes when I can't see her and I'm leaning over too far, slipping, falling,

falling . . . five, ten, twenty metres . . . Oh, God, I'm going to die. Pain, terrible pain as I hit a rock . . . no more pain but I can't move . . . I can't move . . .

'*¡Despierta, despierta! Señor* Osborn, you are having the bad dream!'

It is the Spanish surgeon who operated on me when the *ambulancia* brought me down from Pradollano, the Spanish ski resort in the Sierra Nevada, to the University Hospital Carlos Haya, in Malaga. The same surgeon who told me in excellent English that I have broken my neck and it is touch and go whether I will ever move my limbs again.

I am tired, so tired, but I dare not go back to sleep because I know I'll have that nightmare again.

ONE

Late March

The Alfa Romeo drew to a halt a few yards beyond the pretty old-world cottage in Hook Norton where Antonia's parents, Joan and David Ward, were spending their retirement years. They were not expecting their daughter's visit on this sunny spring day, and were ensconced in basket chairs in front of the open windows of the little conservatory reading their Sunday newspapers.

Justin Metcalf, the young man at the wheel of his beloved sports car, turned to look at the anxious face of the girl he intended to marry.

'Are you absolutely sure this secrecy is necessary, babe? I mean, there's no reason why your parents will think me unsuitable, is there? Dad seems pleased to have me working for him so I'm not likely to be made redundant,' he added with a smile, 'and I earn enough dosh to keep us both in comfort, et cetera, et cetera. And I haven't a stain on my character!' He grinned disarmingly and his dark eyes twinkled, enhancing still further his good looks. 'I mean, my ma and pa are over the moon about you, Toni – said you were just the very girl they would have chosen for me. Ma was a bit disappointed that her precious son would not be having a "proper wedding", as she called it. She'd have liked St Margaret's and ten bridesmaids and the reception at Hampton Court or something.'

With a smile, he leaned over and kissed her cheek, adding: 'Mind you, she's quite taken with the thought that she can tell all her friends how romantic it all is – love at first sight and all that, and how we are so much in love we can't wait to be man and wife!'

Toni returned his smile briefly but then her look of concern returned. She took his hand in hers.

'Justin, we've been over this a dozen times and I thought you understood why I'm concerned. It's different for your parents; they are almost a generation younger than mine and they live a completely different kind of life. Mum and Dad are about as unsophisticated as yours are "with it". They are ultra-conventional – old-fashioned really – and it was difficult enough for them to come to terms with the fact that I'd virtually be leaving home for good when I went off to Leeds University. For weeks on end, they kept saying I was much too young to be living so far from home, mad as that must sound to you. I think my grandmother is more with it than they are. Besides, I know my mum, like yours, would want me to have a white wedding, and all that palaver. She and Dad would hate the thought of a hurried registry office wedding.'

Hearing Justin's sigh, she pressed her cheek to his. 'Don't worry, hon! Just let me go in on my own and break it gently to them. Then, when I come and fetch you, they'll know how much I love you and they'll see what a lovely person you are and maybe see why we don't want to wait . . .'

Justin put his arms round her and pulled her as close as he could. A sudden smile lit up his face after he had kissed her. 'It isn't as if I'd got you pregnant – shot-gun marriage and all that!' He laughed. 'Just don't be away too long, Toni, or my patience will vanish and I shall have to come in and get you!'

He got out of the car and went round to open the passenger door for her. The air was warm, spring-like, and birds were singing and chattering in the cherry tree in front of the Wards' pretty little house. Primroses, celandines and a few early hyacinths filled the flower bed edging the road. A large ginger cat lay curled up on the doorstep, only deigning to move when the young woman walked up the brick path towards the front door.

With a sigh, Justin returned to the car but did not get inside. Instead he leaned against the bonnet, reflecting what an extraordinary thing Fate was. Meeting a girl, falling in love with her and knowing he wanted to spend the rest of his life with her were the very, very last things on his mind when one of his friends, Mike, had introduced him to Toni at a party. In the ensuing six weeks, seeing Toni every spare moment they could be together, he had finally admitted to himself that he had, quite literally, fallen in love at first sight.

Miraculously, it seemed, Toni reciprocated his feelings. When he told her after their fourth night of love-making that he wanted to marry her, she hadn't hesitated in replying that it was what she wanted, too.

Neither of them had had doubts or second thoughts. Everything about their relationship was as if they were two halves of a whole. Both were only children, both had done well academically and in sports: both loved dancing and skiing, and Justin, who was a ten handicap golfer, was over the moon when Toni reported that it was one of the very few activities that her father, once a keen golfer himself, had taught her how to play.

'Let's get married right away – no point in waiting,' Justin had suggested as the weeks went by. He took her to meet his parents, who lived in a fabulous penthouse flat in Grosvenor House. His father, Philip Metcalf, had been enchanted with Toni – so unlike Justin's previous girlfriends, who were all society girls, immensely self-assured and mostly from affluent homes. Toni's quiet, rather shy gentleness had appealed to the older man whose wife, Shelly, was the very reverse. She spent her time beautifying her already beautiful self, and a great deal of money on fashionable clothes, shoes and handbags which made only one or two appearances before disappearing from sight. She was bright, amusing, a first-class bridge player and a good wife who, if she did not exactly worship her husband, certainly worshipped Justin, her good-looking, popular young son. Having met Toni, she was quite delighted and reassured by the fact that the girl was far too unsophisticated ever to try and put her, Justin's adoring mother, on the back burner.

Surely, Justin now thought as he waited for the front door to open and Toni to call him inside, her parents were not going to raise objections? Not that they could prevent the marriage even if they disapproved, but Justin was by no means certain that Toni would go against their wishes. Old fashioned and elderly though they might be, she loved them dearly.

Inside Cherry Tree Cottage, both Joan and David Ward were regarding their daughter with horror. For the third time, Joan Ward was saying, 'But darling, you can't possibly know this young man well enough after less than three months and . . .'

'Mum, four months!' Toni corrected her, trying hard to keep

her voice uncontroversial. 'And I am twenty-three years old and Justin is twenty-eight, so we aren't irresponsible teenagers. Anyway, all I'm asking is that you and Dad meet him, and then make your comments.'

David Ward regarded the flushed face of his only child and said to his wife, 'That's a reasonable request, my dear! After all, Toni is grown up now, and I think we shall all feel a lot happier when we've met the young man. Go and call him in, Toni, whilst your mother makes us all a nice cup of tea.' He put an arm lightly round his daughter's shoulders, adding: 'I don't have to tell you, darling, that we both love you very much, and our only concern is your happiness.'

Far from reassured, Toni went out to the car where Justin was still standing, a questioning look on his face. 'I'm afraid they haven't taken it very well!' she said. 'It's just as I thought it would be: "you haven't known each other long enough". I suppose it does seem a bit quick to them.' She reached up and touched his cheek, adding: 'If the worst comes to the worst, we could just get engaged. We don't have to get married next week, do we?'

She attempted a smile, but Justin's expression was far from happy.

'No, we don't have to, as you say, but what about my plans for our honeymoon? I wasn't going to tell you as I wanted it to be a surprise, but I've booked two weeks at that really cool Spanish golf hotel near Marbella. The dates coincide with your Easter break from that office of yours. When you saw the brochure and said it sounded marvellous if ever we could afford it, I decided to surprise you . . .' He broke off, looking thoroughly dejected.

'Oh, Justin, I know I said it sounded wonderful, and I meant it – but I didn't realize you were going to book it – and so soon. Can't you postpone it . . . till the summer, or something?'

'No!' Justin replied. 'I suppose it was silly of me but I've booked the flights as well as the hotel!' Then his face brightened. 'Even if we can't get married, we can still go on holiday, can't we?'

Toni managed a smile as she hugged him. 'I'm just so sorry about all this, darling. I really am! And your parents made me feel so welcome. Come on, let's go in. I know Mum and Dad will love you.' Linking her arm through his, she walked with him up the path to the front door.

Toni was not wrong in her belief that Joan and David Ward would approve of Justin. 'How could they not?' she said to him afterwards as they drove back to London. They'd insisted they would have nothing – absolutely nothing – against the marriage if the young couple were willing to wait at least until the end of the year. When Justin pointed out apologetically that he had somewhat jumped the gun and booked the honeymoon, they'd done their best to hide their shock but at least they did not raise any objections to the couple enjoying a holiday together.

'You could almost certainly get the hotel to give you two single rooms in place of the honeymoon suite,' Toni's mother suggested innocently. It was the one thing about the whole distressing afternoon that caused Justin to smile as he negotiated the slip road on to the M40 as they drove back to London.

'When your mother suggested single rooms, I understood how out of this modern world they are!' he said. 'I cannot imagine their reactions if they were to know how many hours we've spent making love, if not in your flat then in mine! Never mind, hon, it's very far from the end of the world. I shall buy you a ring and you will wear it and we shall have a breath-taking honeymoon in the bridal suite.'

All Toni's disappointment vanished in an instant as her heart filled with love and gratitude. Justin must have been hurt as well as disappointed by her parents' attitude towards their relationship, but as she had pointed out to him, it was not him they doubted so much as their worry that it was far too soon for her to know her own mind.

Nothing – nothing in the whole wide world, she told herself – could alter the fact that, wedding or no wedding, she belonged to Justin, body and soul, and that she could never love anyone else.

TWO

It was Easter day, Aaron Osborn's fifteenth day in hospital. His whole body was still covered with the bruises he had received when he'd fallen over the edge of the piste. Encased in a plaster cast so that he was unable to move, unable to understand the Spanish conversation coming from the television set at the end of his bed, he had no way to distract himself from memories of the frightening events which had brought him here.

Earlier in the day, the surgeon had warned him that despite the operation he had performed on his neck, the break was perilously close to the part of his spine which controlled movement, and that the slightest displacement could cause further paralysis.

Was he always to be dogged by bad luck? he asked himself bitterly. Two years ago, he'd thought his luck had taken a huge turn for the better the day he had met his future wife, Leena. Until then, although girls fell for his exceptional good looks and tall, athletic figure, as far as he was concerned, the subsequent relationships had been superficial, purely physical. One of the girls had accused him bitterly of being incapable of love, and he had realized this was true.

Aaron's thoughts now winged back to his childhood. The only son of two middle-aged Scots, his upbringing had started in Japan where both his parents taught English in Japanese schools. His arrival in their ordered lives had been unintentional and unwanted, and as soon as he was born, he'd been handed over to a Japanese *nani*.

By the age of six, he was bi-lingual and more inclined to use Japanese customs than those of his parents. At the age of seven, he was taken by his father to England and left with a hitherto unknown bachelor uncle who was to be his unwilling guardian. Packed off to a boarding prep school, he was teased and bullied by the boys his own age, who had quickly recognized his behaviour as different from their own.

Perhaps, Aaron thought now, he would not have achieved such excellent academic results had he been welcomed by his contemporaries. As it was, he'd concentrated upon his studies, his only escape from his loneliness. The pattern had been repeated at his public school, and his relationship with his bachelor uncle remained, by mutual agreement, almost as if they were strangers.

If anything, their relationship had worsened when his parents' quarterly payments for Aaron's keep stopped suddenly when they were killed in the great Hanshin earthquake which devastated the important city of Kobe where they'd lived. Nothing they owned had been insured and only enough money remained, after the earthquake, to pay for the few outstanding debts and for his parents' funerals.

Having seen them only once a year since he'd been sent to England, their deaths when Aaron was twelve years old had not caused him any grief. The reduction of his pocket money had affected him far more, and it had suddenly dawned on him that he would have to find a well-paid job when he left school if he was ever to get the things he wanted. By the time he left his public school with four 'A's at A-level, he had decided to become a lawyer.

During the subsequent three years reading law at university, Aaron had been obliged to take any job available during the holidays in order to fund his needs. His social life, therefore, was almost non-existent. Having obtained a first, on his tutor's recommendation, he decided to complete the remaining years of his training at the London School of Law.

While there, fellow students sometimes included him in their social lives, and Aaron was never without a girlfriend. With his dark hair, unusual grey eyes and tall, perfectly proportioned body, he could easily pick up a girl and discard her if she became too emotionally demanding.

His poverty was a constant source of irritation to him and he had resolved never to get married unless it were to an extremely wealthy wife.

Shortly after his twenty-sixth birthday, Aaron met Leena. He'd been a late addition to a formal dinner party given by a fellow student when one of the expected male guests was unable to attend. Leena Banerjee, the daughter of wealthy Indian parents, was by far the most attractive of the female guests and was seated on his right-hand side at the dinner table. She was not only beautiful but amusing in a sophisticated way, and from her conversation he'd gauged correctly that her parents were extremely wealthy, and that she was their hopelessly indulged only child.

Aaron had responded instantly to her barely disguised interest in him, and a few weeks later they became lovers, Aaron spending a great deal of time in Leena's fabulous king-sized bed in her penthouse flat in Mayfair. When he'd told his insatiable, demanding lover that he could not afford to spend so much time with her because of his studies, she swept such excuses aside and suggested they should get married.

Once he was reasonably certain that it was safe to do so, Aaron confessed his total inability to finance Leena's lifestyle, as he had two more years of studying to do before he could sit his final exams and start earning a living. As he had expected, Leena swept aside such obstacles to her desires, assuring him that her father had settled a huge allowance for her as he adored her and always made certain she had everything she wanted. She would take Aaron out to India to meet her parents, who she was certain would love him as much as she did.

Aaron had raised no objection. He'd always craved the kind of wealthy lifestyle that Leena had made clear she would be able to provide.

The trip to India had been a near disaster, he recalled now. Leena's father threatened to cut off her allowance if she married him, a penniless, jobless law student. However, Leena's threat that she would never speak to her father again if he continued to object to their marriage won his very reluctant agreement to their union. Furthermore, he agreed to provide her with a large enough income to keep her in maximum comfort for the rest of her life.

Aaron's nurse arrived to give him his medication and interrupted his reminiscences, but as soon as she had gone, the memories had come flooding back. He and Leena had only been married for a few months before he'd realized what a dreadful mistake he had made. Leena was as wilful, selfish and demanding as she was beautiful. It was her will to which he must accede even when it conflicted with his own. She expected his full attention at all times, and their day-to-day activities were decided by her, regardless of his wishes and desires.

Inevitably, there were rows, but much as he abhorred their relationship, by the second year of marriage, he had become entirely accustomed to the life of luxury they led. At Leena's insistence he had dropped out of college and never completed his course. He did not need to earn money, she had insisted. She had more than enough for both of them. The daunting thing was that if he tried to divorce her, the hugely generous allowance from her father would almost certainly cease and he would be left with nothing. He now faced the fact that one thing was absolutely certain: Leena did not intend to let him go.

It was then he'd realized that he must try to find some other way to free himself from her domination and regain his freedom.

Aaron's reflections were again interrupted, this time by the surgeon who had operated on him. Arrangements were being made, he was told, for him to be flown back to England, to Stoke Mandeville hospital, when he was fit enough. Fortunately the skiing holiday had been insured, and the costs of his journey back to England would be covered by the insurance company.

The accident that had caused Leena's death and Aaron's injuries was in the hands of the Spanish courts, who had finally released her body. She had been cremated and her ashes taken back to India by her distraught parents.

Although Aaron had been found the same day he had fallen, it was three days before Leena's body was discovered. A party of mountain climbers saw her laying several hundred metres below the rocky ledge which had arrested his own fall and hidden her from view. Now, when the surgeon had departed leaving him alone once more, a familiar depression engulfed him. Would he be able to do anything worthwhile again if, as seemed likely, he ended up a quadriplegic? His surgeon had refused to commit himself even to the possibility of a partial recovery.

Was he being punished by some mythical Higher Being for his wrong-doing? Aaron now asked himself bitterly.

Tears of physical pain as well as mental depression ran down Aaron's handsome face. If he might be confined to a hospital bed for the rest of his life, what good would Leena's money be to him then? They had both made wills shortly before they'd been married, naming each other as beneficiaries – which had seemed ridiculous at the time when he possessed little other than the clothes he stood up in.

His face was distorted with bitterness and fear as now in the lonely hours of the day, as well as in his nightmares, he relived the moments when all his plans had gone so disastrously wrong and he had as good as lost his life.

THREE

Justin slipped a couple of Euros into the waiting porter's hand, and when the smiling hotel servant had left the room, he turned to put his arms round Toni. She was standing looking down through the wall of glass windows at the panorama of a white sandy beach and brilliant blue Mediterranean Sea beyond the picturesque hotel gardens.

As the door closed, she turned and lifted a radiant face to his.

'Oh, Justin, it's beautiful!' she breathed. 'I knew it was going to be lovely from the brochure, but not as . . . as . . .' She broke off as she tried to find adequate adjectives to describe the Hotel Los Palmeros. She had been to Europe before, on package holidays with a group of friends, staying usually in self-catering chalets, and once or twice in small half-board hotels. She had also holidayed once in Cyprus with her late, wealthy godmother – on that occasion in the comparative luxury of a four-star hotel. But this hotel was quite fantastic. The room in which she was standing was large enough to contain a sofa, two armchairs, a glass-topped coffee table, side tables and a refrigerator containing every kind of drink, including a bottle of champagne. On yet another table stood a vast television set with a large notice on the screen saying both in English and Spanish: WELCOME TO THE HOTEL LOS PALMEROS. On top of a writing desk was a huge bouquet of flowers and on a table by one of six floor-to-ceiling windows stood a basket of exotic-looking fruits, beside which were plates, cutlery and white napkins, ready for anyone choosing to eat them.

A few minutes earlier, the porter had carried their suitcases into the beautifully furnished suite. The bedroom contained a huge double bed, a single bed, a wall of built-in cupboards, an ornate dressing table and chairs. The same heavy curtains adorned the sides of the many tall windows, all of which opened on to a wide, tiled balcony containing lounge chairs with comfortable

cushions. Adjoining the bedroom was a bathroom with a bath
and shower against one wall, and a long, tiled washstand with
two basins on the other. Stacked against the wall were two shelves
each containing a pile of white fluffy towels, and from one wall
hung two white towelling bath robes beneath which were two
pairs of white towelling bath slippers. By each basin was a basket
full to overflowing with scented soaps, gels, nail files, sewing
kit, toothbrushes, shower caps and flannels.

'Justin, it's like having our own flat!' Toni exclaimed, her
cheeks flushed, her eyes shining. 'I never imagined it could all
be so . . . so wonderful!'

'I wanted you to like it – I thought you might!' he said, pushing
a wisp of silky light-brown hair from her forehead as his arms
tightened around her. 'I love you – really, really love you, hon!'
he added in a low, husky voice. He smiled suddenly. 'I know we
aren't married but I want this holiday to be like our honeymoon
and for you to be so happy you will never change your mind
about becoming Mrs Justin Anchitel Metcalf.'

Seeing the puzzled expression on Toni's face, he grinned. 'I
know Anchitel sounds odd, which is why I mention it as seldom
as possible. It's an old English Christian name used for sons of
one of my father's ancestors in the sixteenth century. The story
goes that when the fellow died, he said no son could inherit his
not inconsiderable wealth unless he bore the name. God knows
whether that proviso is still valid after all this time, but subsequent generations have not been prepared to risk ignoring it,
including my father. So, whenever you refuse me my marital
rights, I shall refer to you as Mrs Anchitel!'

Toni's eyes glowed with laughter as she replied: 'And our
first son would have to have the name. Meanwhile, Justin
Anchitel Metcalf, I would remind you that I am not yet your
wife, and I shall refuse you your marital rights whenever it
pleases me!'

'Then it had better not be often,' Justin said as his arms tightened around her, 'as I want you most of the time! Ever since we
got on that wretched plane at Gatwick and sat cramped side by
side, I've been wanting to make love to you. I swear to God we
aren't going economy class again, whatever you say about wasting
money. It's not as if I can't afford a few luxuries.'

'Justin, a few!' Toni repeated. 'What about this hotel? Are you really that well off? You never told me you were rich!'

Justin shrugged. 'Guess I wanted you to love me for myself, not my bank account! Anyway, I did tell your father I had a secure job and could keep you in moderate comfort.'

Toni drew in her breath, a quizzical look on her face as she pointed to their luxurious surroundings. 'So this is "moderate comfort", is it? All I can say is if "moderate comfort" means something is lacking, I'd like to know what it is.'

Justin's reply was instantaneous. 'I want you, Toni – right now, on that big bed you were admiring – or better still, on the small one. I love you, far too much for my own good, I dare say!' He gave a brief smile as he added: 'I suppose you are getting fed up hearing me say that so often, but I do really love you.'

He released her suddenly and went over to the refrigerator to take out the bottle of champagne. Pouring two glasses, he handed one to Toni, and putting his other arm around her, he said, 'Having you here – with me, like this . . . it's like a dream come true. I never imagined love – real love – could be like this.'

Toni smiled up at him, her eyes dancing. 'Justin, you told me that not long ago you'd been madly in love with Poppy – the girl with the stable full of show horses, that you shared a flat with her for nearly two years. How can you say you didn't know what being in love was like?'

Justin pulled her down on to the sofa and raised his glass to her before drinking from it. 'I truly believed I was in love with Poppy. How was I to know it could be like this? I've only got to be within sight of you and I'm wanting to make love to you, and it's not just that. I love the way you look, the way your eyes crinkle when you smile, the things you say, the way your nose turns sideways . . .'

'Justin, it doesn't!' Toni cried, putting down her glass and punching him lightly in the chest. 'Just because I told you I'd broken my nose when I fell off the swing when I was five, it doesn't mean it's deformed. And anyway, you've got a crooked front tooth!'

Laughing, he put down his glass beside hers and took her in his arms. 'There you go!' he said enigmatically. 'You only have to scowl at me like that to set my heart thumping. Come on, let's make use of that nice big bed in there.'

As Toni followed him through the arch into the bedroom, it flashed through her mind what an extraordinary thing was Fate. It was quite by chance she had been invited to a girlfriend's wedding. They had never been particularly close and she nearly opted not to go. But she had gone, and it was there the bride's father had introduced her to Justin, one of the four ushers. He was looking remarkably handsome in his grey striped trousers and black morning coat over a pale grey waistcoat. The fact that his shirt and shoes were handmade was something she only discovered some weeks later when he'd asked her if she could find a moment in her lunch hour to pop into Crockett & Jones in Jermyn Street to order a new pair of golf shoes to be made for him.

Far from influencing her in Justin's favour, Toni had been slightly intimidated by her girlfriend's assurances that he was one of the most popular and eligible young bachelors 'still up for grabs' as she'd put it, and Toni should be over the moon that he had taken a shine to her.

'Grab him, sweetie!' Fiona had said. 'He's far too good looking – and nice, too – to hold out for freedom much longer!'

'Justin!' she said now, her eyes thoughtful. 'I know you believe you love me, and I believe it, too, but how can either of us be sure it will last? After all, you fell out of love with Poppy just as I fell out of love with my ex. Suppose . . . well, suppose we go ahead and get married, what if you wake up one morning wanting to be with someone else?'

For once, Justin did not reply. He was too busy undressing her and himself. Flinging back the gold damask bed cover, he pulled her down beside him and began to make love to her.

It was very far from the first time they had made love, but this time, Toni thought, it was somehow different – almost as if they were truly one and not two individuals loving one another. As always, Justin was a passionate but considerate lover who was anxious for her pleasure to be as complete and satisfying as his own. As she lay beside him, her heartbeat gently slowing, Justin's flushed face against her shoulder, she knew she had never in the whole of her life been happier – or more certain

that she wanted to be his wife and spend the rest of her life with
him.

Twenty minutes later, after she had unpacked her suitcase, she
lay in the big bath Justin had filled for her, beneath a cloud of
soap bubbles, her head turned to watch Justin standing naked
with his back to her whilst he shaved at one of the basins. She
could imagine her hands on that slim muscled torso as he lifted
his arms, running her fingers through his fair hair where it curled
into the nape of his neck. She recalled the huskiness of his
voice when they'd lain entwined after their love-making, vowing
once again his love for her.

She was about to speak to him when through the closed bathroom
door she heard voices in their salon. Justin heard them too, and
his face broke into a wide grin.

'Girls have come to turn down the beds and tidy up!' he said.
'We can't have heard them knock. I can't wait to see their faces
when they come in to tidy the bathroom and see us both starkers!'

Toni was about to protest when the bathroom door, which they
had not troubled to lock, was opened by one of the two Spanish
maids, her arms piled with folded towels balanced precariously
over another basket of bathroom toiletries. Her eyes went from
Toni's face above the bath foam to Justin's naked body and she
broke into a torrent of Spanish.

'*Perdone, perdone, Señor, Señora!*' she said. '*No sabe . . .* no
know *señors presenciar!*'

'*Cincuenta minutos!*' Justin told her, smiling. '*No preoccupada!*'
He held out five fingers and repeated that they could return in
fifty minutes.

After they had gone, he held one of the bath sheets for Toni
to wrap around herself as she came out of the bath and his eyes
were alight with laughter.

'Half an hour earlier and they would have found us *in flagrante
delicto!*'

Toni reached up and kissed him. 'You're a sadist, Justin Metcalf.
I do believe you would have enjoyed those poor women's discomfiture. I shall make sure the door is locked in future.'

Justin laughed again, and then looked at his watch lying on
the side of the basin. 'Quarter to seven, hon. By the time we're
dressed the restaurant will be open for dinner. I'm starving! That

horrible ham sandwich they gave us on the plane was even worse than the plastic carton of trifle – if that's what it was!'

Toni wrapped the towel more tightly around her and walked barefoot to one of the big spacious cupboards in which she had hung her clothes. Justin had warned her that occasionally on a Saturday night, long evening dress was still worn, but that for the most part she would only need a short one.

'Anything, really!' he'd told her in a particularly casual, masculine way. 'But not jeans, of course!'

Toni had taken advice from her boss, Julia Nilson, the extremely smart beauty editor of *Temptation* magazine, for whom Toni worked as a PA. She had spent a chunk of her savings on three expensive dresses – not her usual off-the-peg choices. She now selected her favourite one – a short Amanda Wakeley number with a cleverly cut gored skirt that swirled round her knees when she moved. Justin had given her a silver chain and pendant necklace, and the lime-green stones exactly matched the material of the silk chiffon dress. She had determined that Justin would be nothing but proud of her on this special holiday that he had planned with such care and enthusiasm.

'Ties are no longer compulsory!' he was saying now as he pulled on one of his white shirts. 'Think I'll wear one all the same. I can always take it off if it gets too hot. Get a bit better service from the head waiter if you're decently turned out. Actually, he already knows I'll give him a decent something at the end of our stay. The staff here do extremely well from tips. Reckon some of my jobless chums should apply for work in a place like this. It's what I'd do if I had to.'

When Toni went down in the lift, her arm was tucked firmly in Justin's, and when they walked into the dining room she did her best not to appear as impressed as she was. The big room was softly lit but there were small individual lights on each table. The tables were covered in snow-white cloths, barely to be seen beneath a mass of glasses in different sizes and shapes. One exotic orchid in a slender crystal vase provided the centrepiece. On the larger oblong tables, these accoutrements were repeated down their length.

Toni glimpsed Justin slip something into the head waiter's hand as he came forward to greet them.

'We'd like to be by the window – not too close to the music,' Justin said. 'My wife and I are here for two weeks and we would like the same table to be available for us.'

'Certainly, *Señor*,' the man replied, his English accent almost perfect. 'I will see that it is reserved for you. Please, follow me!'

The restaurant was almost full despite the comparatively early hour of eight o'clock. Spaniards tended to dine more frequently at nine or ten, having enjoyed siestas during the day and not returning to their offices until later in the evening.

They made their way past the crowded tables to the one Justin had requested. The head waiter swept back Toni's chair for her before ensuring Justin was also comfortably seated.

'I will send the sommelier with the wine list to you immediately, *Señor*, and the waiter will be here in a moment to take your orders. I will leave these with you.' He then gave each of them a thin red leather-bound folder containing both an à la carte menu and the restaurant's choices for the evening.

When Justin had given his request to the wine waiter, and they had chosen what they wished to eat, he reached across the table and took Toni's hand in his.

'Happy?' he asked, unnecessarily, as her face was shining with almost childish delight.

Before she could reply, the orchestra, which had been playing a Spanish song with which they were both unfamiliar, suddenly started playing 'This Guy's in Love With You', a song made famous by Herb Alpert in the sixties. Justin had given Toni the CD when they had heard it sung by Noel Gallagher recently.

Toni leaned across the table and grabbed Justin's hand. 'Our song, Justin, they're playing our song!'

Regardless of the other diners in the room, in an old-fashioned gesture she never forgot, Justin raised her hand to his lips. A waiter suddenly appeared at Toni's side and put a plate in front of her containing a perfect single red rose with a ring round the stem and a tiny card saying, in Spanish, *I love you!*

The smartly dressed middle-aged lady at the adjoining table had obviously observed the incident and was smiling as she said to Justin in broken English: 'You are *luna de miel* – how is it you say, 'oneymoon? My husband and I wish you *félicitations*.'

Toni blushed but Justin was smiling.

'My wife and I are most grateful for your good wishes!' he said. 'This is our first evening here, and we are looking forward to playing golf tomorrow.'

At once, the woman's husband broke into a torrent of Spanish which his wife did her best to translate, explaining that he was once a professional golfer in his youth and could recommend the most enjoyable courses in the environs of the hotel where they might play.

The waiter had now arrived to serve them their delicious-looking starters and conversation with their neighbours ceased.

Toni looked at Justin. 'I wish we really were on our honeymoon – that I was your wife. I love you so much, and I'm so grateful for everything . . . for this.' She picked up the rose and gently eased the ring from the stem. It was a perfect single diamond encircled by a cluster of tiny ones set in platinum.

Justin reached across the table and, taking the ring from her, slipped it over her finger, saying, 'I've wanted to give you an engagement ring ever since you said you would marry me but it took longer to make than the jeweller had expected.' He gave her a disarming smile. 'I suppose as you are masquerading as my wife, you ought to have a wedding ring on, too!'

'Oh, Justin, it's beautiful! Really lovely,' she said huskily. She looked at his face, as radiant as she suspected was her own.

She saw the delight he was feeling at her response as he muttered, 'Glad you like it, hon!' He raised his glass of wine. 'To us!'

Much as Toni had been looking forward to this two-week holiday in Spain with Justin, she had never once imagined that it would be so perfect, so romantic. She had described him to her girlfriends as a lovely, good-looking, straightforward, regular kind of guy. That he was capable of such romantic gestures as arranging for the band to play their special song, the beautiful rose, the fantastic ring, had never crossed her mind, nor the wonderful honeymoon suite. Such gestures, she would have said, happened in books and films – not in real life.

After they had finished their meal and gone down to the dimly lit bar, they sat drinking coffee and liqueurs and holding hands.

A couple of a similar age to themselves came in and sat down at the adjoining table. Although of Portuguese nationality, they spoke near-perfect English and were soon in friendly conversation. They proceeded to describe at length the wonderful day's skiing they had enjoyed at Borreguiles up in the Sierra Nevada mountains. To Toni's and Justin's surprise, they were told it was only a few hours' drive away.

Justin, a keen skier, was intrigued that there was still snow so far south as late as April.

'It is melting fast!' he was told. 'And the lower slopes were bare, but high up it is still possible to have good skiing. You can hire skis, boots and helmet for the day if you wish.'

'Only one of the black runs is closed,' his wife added. 'Not for bad snow but a few weeks ago an English lady was killed falling from the edge of the piste down into the ravine. Her husband fell too but some rocks saved him from so deep a fall. Other pistes are not dangerous.'

'We must have a day there!' Justin said enthusiastically to Toni. 'I never knew you could ski in Spain so far south! Shows how ignorant I am.'

When Toni reminded him that she had only ever been skiing on two occasions with some university friends he told her she would be perfectly safe with him and that they would stay on the easy slopes.

At that moment, five musicians came into the bar and set up their instruments beside the edge of the small dance floor that occupied the centre of the room. Within minutes, they were playing dance music, their repertoire including English and American popular hits. By mutual agreement, conversation between the two couples ceased and Justin was on the dance floor, his arms holding Toni closely to him as the vocalist sang one of their favourite songs. Stopping only once to say goodnight to the Portuguese couple who retired early, they continued dancing until nearly midnight, when they retired to their exotic bedroom, exhausted.

When Justin finally climbed into bed beside Toni, he drew a long, contented sigh. 'Having you here with me makes everything quite perfect,' he said. 'As you know, I was really looking forward to the golf and swimming, but I never guessed we could go skiing, too. We'll go the day after tomorrow, shall we, hon? We will play golf tomorrow.'

Toni nodded as she said drowsily, 'Yes, we will, tomorrow . . .'
Her voice trailed into silence as sleep overcame her. Smiling,
Justin drew her even closer into his arms and within minutes he,
too, was asleep.

FOUR

Despite the late hour at which Justin and Toni had gone to sleep, they were tempted out of bed by the warm, golden sunshine streaming through the big picture windows.

'Wonderful morning for our golf!' Justin said as he busied himself by making them both a cup of tea. 'You do feel up to it, don't you, darling?'

Toni smiled. 'Doubt I could walk eighteen holes but I could about manage to complete the course in a buggy!'

Justin grinned. 'I can tell you something, hon – if we play golf, make love and dance like that every night, I shall have to be flown home on a stretcher!' He handed her a large, bone-china cup of tea, and added, 'Not to worry about the buggy. They're used a lot out here – gets people moving round the course quicker than walking, which means they can accommodate more golfers so they make more money! Most of the good courses at this time of the year are so crowded you have to book in advance.'

He began to rummage in his suitcase for shorts and T-shirt. 'Good thing Reception managed to book a starting time for us this morning.'

Toni put down her empty teacup, walked to the windows overlooking the hotel gardens and the Olympic-sized swimming pool and said, 'It would be really cool to come back here after the golf and chill out down there by the pool and get ourselves a tan!'

Justin nodded. 'We've got two whole weeks to do that, and I daresay we'll both get sunburnt up the mountain when we ski. We must buy some high-altitude cream.'

He broke off briefly whilst he struggled into his clothes, then said, 'Breakfast is fantastic here – you'll love it! It's a colossal help-yourself buffet, and I've yet to think of a single thing one might want which isn't available – every type of bread, meat, fish, cereal, fruit. There's a chef with a hot plate who will cook anything you fancy – omelette, poached eggs, fried bread – you name it! It's fun, too, as you get to talk to the other guests as you move round the long buffet tables.'

Toni turned to look at Justin curiously. 'I know you said you'd been to this hotel before, in the days when your parents spent every Easter in Spain before it became too touristy. Has it changed since then?'

'Indeed it has!' Justin told her. 'All the rooms have been modernized and now there's a second swimming pool and a Jacuzzi, and the big garden restaurant where we have breakfast and lunch. The dining room we were in last night is only open at night.'

'So you've been here since you were a child?'

For a split second, Justin hesitated before saying as casually as he could: 'I've been golfing here with the boys . . .' He broke off, having no wish to upset Toni by saying that he had once brought out a girlfriend for a long weekend. The assignation had not, as it happened, been a success, but at the time he'd thought what a cool place it would be to take a girl he fancied. Almost as soon as he'd met Toni and known he wanted to marry her, he'd thought of bringing her here to this hotel. He'd decided it best not to mention the previous unsatisfactory assignation for fear of Toni's reactions.

Instead, he told her that he had been to the hotel before with his golfing friends. Toni was now so attuned to every nuance of Justin's voice that she found herself wondering what exactly had happened on that 'boys' holiday', as he'd called it. Maybe they had all got very drunk, she decided, and disgraced themselves somehow. And yet he had been greeted with immense pleasure when they'd checked in – smiles and enthusiastic welcomes from all the staff. Maybe they were as a result of him being such a lavish tipper, she told herself.

Justin's casual attitude to money was something to which she had not yet grown accustomed. He always seemed to have more than enough for his needs and would never allow her to chip in her share. He was also prone to buying her presents, to the extent that she had to take care not to admire anything in a shop window or he would march straight in and buy it for her.

She was reminded now about the beautiful ring he had given

her in the restaurant the night before, and was pleased that Justin had locked it away in the small safe which was concealed in one of the four wardrobes. It was certainly not something she dared risk losing on a golf course.

'Stop dreaming and get a move on, slowcoach!' Justin said, crossing the room to stand behind her whilst she brushed her hair. 'Why do women take so long beautifying themselves? You're pretty enough without make-up, hon.' He dropped a kiss on top of her head, adding: 'I'm absolutely starving!'

As soon as they entered the huge sunny breakfast room, a waiter hurried towards them and showed them to a vacant table overlooking the swimming pool. Already there were people swimming, and many of the lounge chairs bordering the pool were occupied with sun worshippers.

Watching Toni's face, Justin felt a warm glow of pleasure. He had so much wanted her to enjoy the luxury of the hotel he had chosen for the honeymoon they'd not been able to celebrate. He was well aware that her elderly parents were not, and had never been, very well off, although they had managed to send Toni to a good school and they had borrowed the money for her university fees. Her father, now in his sixties, had taken early retirement and arthritis had made it impossible for her mother to continue working as a hospital nurse. A hotel such as this would never, therefore, have been within their means. As a consequence it was a double joy – to have Toni entirely to himself for two whole weeks, and to enjoy watching her reaction to the luxurious surroundings.

Toni was now laughing as Justin drew her over to the heavily laden buffet tables, which served English dishes as well as global specialities she'd never tried before.

'If you put one more thing on my plate, I shall opt out of golf this morning,' she threatened as Justin heaped yet another delicacy on her plate. 'One thing is certain: I won't want any lunch!'

'Wait and see!' Justin replied as he carried their plates past the other diners to their table. 'They serve lunch at three o'clock out here, so by then you might be hungry again after all eighteen holes of golf.'

'Exercise! In a buggy?' Toni said, smiling as a waiter placed a coffee pot and milk jug in front of them, saying in excellent English that they had only to call him if they required more.

'Oh, Justin, it's all so . . . so perfect!' Toni exclaimed as she filled their cups. 'All of it, our beautiful room, the dinner last night, the dancing . . . and now this . . .'

She broke off, aware that Justin was not listening but was poised holding his knife and fork above his plate, staring across the room. At the same time, there was a subtle increase in the hum of conversation in the huge room. Toni turned her head to follow his gaze, as every other diner was doing. The head waiter was ushering in two newcomers, leading them to a table which had obviously been reserved for them by the windows overlooking the flower filled garden. A short, heavily built man and a much taller, voluptuous female were now seating themselves at the table.

Justin's voice was hushed as he exclaimed: 'My God! Have you ever seen anyone like that before! Awesome! I wonder who she is . . .'

The Spaniard at the table adjoining theirs had overheard Justin's comment. 'The lady is Carmellia del Concordia, *Señor*!' he said, smiling. 'Our most *famoso* Spanish *estrella* for the films, no?'

Nodding his thanks for the information, Justin turned briefly to Toni. 'Some film star! Puts Angelina Jolie in the shade!'

The film star was indeed quite spectacular, Toni thought as she watched the flurry of activity as a slim blond youth joined them and two waiters settled them into their chairs. The newcomer's boyish good looks, accentuated by long, dark lashes outlining pale, sky-blue eyes, made it obvious he was far younger than the film star, and although he bore no resemblance to her, Toni supposed he might be her son.

'Reckon he's her toy-boy!' Justin was saying. 'She must be well into her forties, if not older; but what a stunner, Toni!' Their table was close enough for them to see the film star's glittering transparent gold gauze caftan, beneath which was a shiny gold bikini, the top barely covering her voluptuous breasts. Her strikingly long legs were covered from the knee downward by gold, gladiator-type lacing to high-heeled sandals. Her toenails as well as her long fingernails were also painted gold, and huge gold earrings framed her deeply tanned, heart-shaped face. Securing her black hair was a gold gauze turban.

Justin was now grinning. 'No wonder everyone is staring,' he

exclaimed. 'She's absolutely stunning. Mind you, those voluptuous curves will doubtless become rolls of fat in a few years'
time. Latin women all seem to put on mountains of fat in their
old age.'

'I suppose as she's a film star, it's in order for her to draw so
much attention to herself,' Toni replied. She pointed to yet another
man who had seated himself nearby. 'That must be her bodyguard
at the next table. He looks like a member of the Mafia!'

Justin laughed. 'I dare say she does need protection – from
rampant males! She looks pretty bored with her toy boy. I think
he may have bitten off a bit more than he can chew – or more
likely, she is about to swallow him whole and spit him out later,
poor kid!'

One of the waiters was now asking if he could bring her
breakfast to her, but she was shaking her head. Not without a
certain grace, she rose to her feet and wound her way through
the tables of goggle-eyed diners, and passed within a foot of
Justin and Toni's table. For a brief instant, she paused, stared
from Justin to Toni and back to Justin again, before sailing past
towards the buffet tables, leaving a lingering waft of expensive
scent behind her.

Turning to look at Justin's face, Toni exclaimed: 'I think she
did a double take just now, darling; she fancied you! Not that
that surprises me – you're a lot better looking than the sad-looking
toy boy. Seems he isn't being allowed to get himself any breakfast
yet!' She broke off, realizing suddenly that Justin had not heard
a word she'd said. He was watching the voluptuous, gold-clad
film star as she acknowledged the greetings of fascinated would-
be breakfasters who stood back so she could have first choice.

'I suppose she is accustomed to all that deference!' Justin said.
'She certainly knows how to make the most of the impact on us
insignificant mortals! Wonder if she'll come back past our table
or go round the other way.'

Justin need not have had any doubts. Carrying a plateful of
exotic salads and crab claws, she paused deliberately at their
table. 'The waiter tells me you English peoples!' she said in
heavily accented English. 'I wish you the 'appy *vacaciones* in my
country!'

By now, Justin had risen politely to his feet but she waved a heavily jewelled hand at his chair, saying, '*Hasta la vista!*' as she glided away to her own table.

'What on earth was that all about?' Toni asked.

Justin looked flushed. 'Oh, it's a sort of Spanish goodbye – well, "until we meet again" kind of thing.'

Toni was trying not to laugh. 'I do believe she fancies you! Pity we can't ask her to join us this morning. Somehow I don't think there's much likelihood she plays golf!'

'Idiot!' Justin replied, and looked at his watch. 'Time we are off if you've finished, hon. They can be quite strict at some of these golf clubs so we need to be on the tee at least ten minutes before play-off time.'

Carmellia del Concordia was forgotten by them both as they played the first nine holes on the magnificent eighteen-hole Golf das Águilas course. Although neither played too well at first, it wasn't long before Justin had regained his top form and Toni had mastered her putting if not all of her drives. The sky was a brilliant, cloudless blue and the scent of the pine trees in the hills above the course was almost over-powering. There was no sign of the eagles after which the course had been named, however.

They had time for a short break at the ninth hole where a slight queue had formed. Justin bought cooling drinks from the man who served them from the refrigerator in the buggy he used to circulate the course for the benefit of thirsty golfers. A couple of similar age to themselves was among those waiting to play off next in line. The man turned to Justin and said in English: 'We saw you both playing the eighth and think we're about the same standard. The pro suggested you might care to let us join up with you?' He smiled as he added: 'We hadn't booked a starting time, so being anxious not to have to turn us away he pointed out that, as a foursome, you'd get round a bit quicker than by yourselves.'

They exchanged information about their respective handicaps and within minutes introductions had been made. While they awaited their turn to drive off the tenth, Toni and Justin discovered that their new acquaintances were also staying at the Hotel Los Palmeros – not in the hotel itself but in one of the apartments in the grounds which shared the hotel facilities.

'Gemma and I come out every year for a couple of months,'

Peter Stonehouse told them. 'Luckily for us, we can take time off when we want as I'm an author and my wife is an illustrator. It does us both good, being sedentary workers, to have some healthy exercise, and you know what the English weather is like. Our golf course at home was closed due to flooding for six months last year!'

Gemma Stonehouse, a friendly woman with carrot-coloured hair and the white skin and freckles that went with it, was delighted to be playing golf with someone of her own standard.

'Have you seen our celebrity yet?' she enquired with a smile. 'Peter calls her the Gold Star! He says she may not have earned a medal at the Olympic Games but certainly ought to have a gold star in the glamour stakes. He's going to put her – disguised, of course – in his next book!'

The two men now drove off, followed by the girls, and all four moved down the fairway, their new partners sharing the buggies.

'The Gold Star and her husband – that's the old man – usually come out for Easter,' Gemma was saying. 'That's if she's not away filming on location.'

Toni looked puzzled. 'I knew the Italians made films – who can forget Sophia Loren? But I've never heard of a Spanish film.'

Gemma laughed. 'Then you should turn on the TV in your bedroom,' she said. 'There's nearly always a film of some sort showing, if not one of passion then a cliff-hanger bull fight!'

Having played their second shots, they resumed their conversation. When Toni heard that the Stonehouses came out to Spain for two or three months every year to avoid the coldest months in England, she understood why Gemma was so well-informed about the hotel's occupants.

'Did you say Carmellia Whatsit – the Gold Star,' she corrected herself, smiling, 'is the wife of that fat man at her table? Then who is the fair-haired boy we saw at breakfast with her?'

Gemma laughed. 'Yes, the old one is the film director who "discovered" her and made her a star. The boy is her latest toy boy. There is usually a different one every time she comes here. The last one had red curly hair like mine! But they are always "youths" as Peter calls them. The husband is at least seventy, which is why, presumably, he turns a blind eye to the toy boys.

Keeps her happy and he knows she'll never leave him. You'll see the old boy from time to time being pushed around in a wheelchair by an attendant. He always appears at breakfast, sometimes at lunch – but never for dinner in the restaurant at night. He comes to the Hotel Los Palmeros mostly for the health treatments in the spa. Carmellia gets all her beauty treatments, hairdressing and so on done there, too. The old man, her husband, is a pretty well-known Spanish film director – that's how she got to be the fairy at the top of the tree.'

'But doesn't the husband mind about the toy boy?' Toni asked.

Gemma shook her head. 'Seems he's quite happy to have her off his hands, so to speak. I'm told he adores her and gives her anything in the world she wants. Hence all that gold what-have-you around her arms and neck. It's all real, twenty-four-carat stuff. That's partly why she has a minder.'

Toni smiled. 'Well as long as she doesn't want Justin,' she said, and related the incident in the dining room that morning. 'She only glanced briefly at me and the rest of the time she was gazing at him.'

Gemma laughed again. 'Best watch out then! Rumour has it she eats men after she's had her proverbial way with them – like the tarantula spider, or is it the black widow? I can never remember!'

Justin seemed to have found Peter Stonehouse as genial company as Toni was finding Gemma, and she had only the tiniest moment of regret when Justin invited the couple to join them in the Orchis bar for drinks that evening.

'The porter told me it was a special night because Las Luciérnigas, a very special four-piece orchestra, would be providing music for dancing and they have a particularly good vocalist.'

By the time they had putted out on the eighteenth green, the foursome had become very good friends.

'Gemma was anxious we shouldn't miss Las Luciérnigas,' Peter said as they returned the buggies and carried their golf bags to their parked cars. 'We heard them last year and my darling wife described the vocalist as – and I quote – "a real heartthrob" – all deep voice and flashing eyes! Not quite my cup of tea!'

'I never said he was a heartthrob,' Gemma said, smiling. 'I simply said he was a really good vocalist and quite romantic!'

'Well, as far as I'm concerned, he might as well have been singing football supporters' songs for all we could understand his passionate Spanish outpourings,' Peter said, and they all laughed once more as Gemma accused her loving husband of being tone deaf.

They parted company as they eased their way out of the crowded car park and drove back to the hotel.

'I really liked both of them,' Justin commented. They had decided to skip lunch, and instead they changed into their swimming gear and went down to the pool. He linked his arm through Toni's and pressed her hand in his own.

'Just let's not get *too* friendly,' he said. 'I don't want to have to share you too often. Selfish git, aren't I?'

Toni returned the pressure of his hand, her cheeks flushed. 'I don't want to share you either!' she told him. 'And if that Carmellia What's-her-name starts ogling you again at dinner the way she did at breakfast, you can tell her to get lost!'

Justin laughed. 'Didn't know you cared!' he teased.

'Well, you are the right build for a toy boy!' Toni replied, pointing to his lean but muscular body.

Laughing, she dumped her beach bag and her large white towel on to one of the waiting lounge chairs and, without waiting for Justin, she jumped into the warm water of the shimmering blue pool. A minute later, Justin was there beside her, holding her by the shoulders as the water lapped around them.

'One more remark like that and I'll dunk you,' he threatened.

'You'll do no such thing, toy boy!' she retorted and, in a flash, had freed herself and darted away in a fast crawl.

'Oh, dear!' said a rather plump lady in a white bikini to her skinny husband. 'I'm afraid that young couple are quarrelling already. She was calling him rude names, and now he's going after her.'

'Don't be silly!' her husband said with a sigh. 'Anyone with a few more brains than you, my dear, would realize that they are very much in love.'

FIVE

While they were dressing for dinner that night, Toni found herself wishing that Justin had not invited the Stonehouse couple to join them in the Orchis bar. Much as she had liked them, Gemma in particular, she wanted Justin all to herself. If she had ever had any doubts at all that she was in love with him, they now vanished as she watched him wrestling with the tie he had decided, regretfully, that he must wear for such a formal dining room.

Mirroring her thoughts, Justin turned and smiled at her. 'You look good enough to eat in that floaty thing you're wearing,' he said. 'If I wasn't so hungry I'd suggest we order something from room service and spend the evening in bed!'

Toni smiled. 'And you'd be none too pleased if I took you up on that suggestion,' she said. 'We didn't have any lunch, remember? And it's now eight o'clock. I thought it was supposed to be women who took so long getting ready!'

Later, after they had finished what had been a fabulous meal, they made their way downstairs to the Orchis bar.

'I've eaten too much!' Justin was saying as a waiter hurried forward to lead them to a table opposite the bar. Justin ordered Toni her favourite absinthe and a brandy for himself.

'What time do the musicians start playing?' he asked the waiter, who replied that they would arrive at ten o'clock. Before that time, many people would still be in the dining room enjoying their dinner.

'Tonight you have good fortune, you understand,' he added as he placed their drinks in front of them. 'In the hotel is our famous Spanish star of the films. She has very beautiful voice and is possible she sing.'

After he had departed, Justin turned with a smile to Toni. 'Seems our gold-clad Carmellia del whatever can sing as well as act,' he said.

Before Toni could reply, they were joined by the Stonehouses,

and by the time their drinks had arrived, the musicians had
appeared and set up their instruments at the far end of the room.
The dance music they now chose to play was fairly cosmopolitan,
the words of the English numbers usually translated into Spanish.

Like the well-mannered gentleman he was, Justin took Gemma
on to the crowded dance floor for a samba, but Peter Stonehouse
excused himself, telling Toni that unfortunately he was tone deaf
and Gemma had forbidden him ever to subject an unfortunate
partner to such misery as dancing with him. Instead, they stayed
chatting amiably about the facilities close to the hotel. He named
several small Spanish restaurants where they could get a light
lunch or dine out as an alternative to eating in the hotel, and
recommended some good shops, a supermarket in Marbella, and
places of exceptional beauty or interest which she and Justin
should visit. He and Gemma did not stay very long, however, as
they wanted an early night.

As they got up to leave, there was a sudden commotion in the
doorway and Carmellia del Concordia sailed into the room. She was
followed by the fair-haired youth and, at a slight distance behind
them, her swarthy bodyguard. There was no sign of her husband.

Toni and Justin sat watching with interest the flurry of activity
caused by the film star's presence. While two waiters scurried
to prepare a table for her on the opposite side of the dance floor
to their own, a third was ushering her to the bar. She draped
herself on one of the tall stools, patting the seat beside her for
the young man who was looking flushed and slightly self-
conscious in a white tuxedo. Carmellia ignored him as she
accepted the glass of champagne now being offered to her by
the senior barman.

She looked, Toni said to Justin, almost majestic. Her full-length
evening gown was a tight-fitting, creamy coloured raw silk creation,
the skirt slit on one side to her thigh, the décolletage so low that
her cleavage, showing a dark golden tan, was almost to her waist.
Round her neck was an astonishingly beautiful diamond necklace
reaching to a point between her ample breasts. Her jet-black hair
had been coiled into a chignon on the back of her head, and
diamond earrings dangled from her ears almost to her shoulders.
Her eyes, black as coal, were heavily outlined and fringed with
long lashes.

'A bit OTT, don't you think?' Justin said. 'Although as a film star, I suppose she needs to look exotic and sexy.'

They both watched as she and the young man were shown to their table where an ice bucket was now standing containing another bottle of champagne, which the waiter opened and poured into the shining flutes. Carmellia now looked slowly round the room and, without embarrassment, sized up the other occupants. Her eyes alighted on Justin and Toni's table and, smiling, she raised her glass to them.

'She must think she knows us!' Justin whispered to Toni.

'*Wants* to know us, you mean!' Toni corrected him. 'It's you she remembers from the breakfast room this morning. I told you she fancied you!'

Justin's reply was drowned out by the noise of the male vocalist singing a Spanish song. The woman sitting on the banquette at the next table leaned across and said, 'You are English guests, I think, and perhaps do not know that this is the song which made Carmellia famous, so he sings for her. He has a very good voice, no?'

Before Toni could reply, the male vocalist went over to the film star's table and held out the microphone to her. There was a brief flurry at the table and then she rose and followed him back to the dais where the musicians were concluding the song, and addressed them. She then took the microphone from the vocalist and turned to face the room, a smile curving her wide, scarlet mouth as the guests broke into enthusiastic applause. She nodded briefly at the waiting musicians, who broke into the introduction to the song 'Crazy for You', and her deep, husky voice filled the room. People had crowded into the bar from the adjoining lounge and stood in the doorways. Not a person moved; all eyes were on the film star as she sang the song.

'She really is quite something!' Justin whispered to Toni, at which point Carmellia turned her head and, looking directly at him, sang the words, '*Solo por tu.*'

Justin flushed as everyone in the room turned to look at him curiously. Toni did her best to smile, but when the song ended and Carmellia, to a long round of applause, returned to her table, she said to Justin: 'I'm sure she doesn't mean to be so . . . so obvious – flirting with you, I mean! It's pretty rude seeing as you are clearly here with me. I do feel sorry for that poor boy she is with; she totally ignores him.'

'He seems happy enough to me!' Justin said wryly. 'That must be the third glass of champagne he's drunk already. Heaven help him if she asks him to dance!'

But it wasn't the youthful blond Swedish boy she asked to dance. When the band started to play the song once more, she scribbled something on one of the paper napkins on their table and beckoned to a hovering waiter. With a quizzical expression, he came over to Justin's table and handed the note to him, saying, 'From *Señora* Carmellia, *Señor!*'

It would please me to have this dance with you, if your lady permits!

'Blow me!' Justin exclaimed, handing the note to Toni. 'Can't really refuse, can I?'

Toni caught her breath. She was familiar with the song which Madonna had recorded and made famous a long time ago and, watching Carmellia stare right at Justin as she sang about how attracted she was to him, she thought that the woman could not have made it any more obvious that she fancied Justin. She probably wanted him as a lover as she was obviously bored with her youthful toy boy. It was equally clear that Justin was willing to dance with her. Toni caught her breath. Could she ask him not to do so? If she did, it would indicate that she didn't trust him.

As casually as she could, she said, 'Enjoy yourself!'

Looking slightly self-conscious, Justin made his way past the other tables and approached Carmellia.

She stood up, smiling. 'I see you dance with your *esposa muy bien*,' she said. 'I like you dance so with me.'

She was, Justin thought as he guided her on to the dance floor and they started to dance, surprisingly light on her feet considering she was a voluptuous woman and could hardly be called lightweight. As they moved, and the male vocalist began to sing the song in English, Carmellia pressed herself tightly against him, a quizzical smile in her large dark brown, almost black eyes, as if, Justin thought, she was inviting him to respond. He was conscious that every eye in the room was on them, not least that of the hapless young man who had been left alone at their table. He was also conscious that this was a lot more than dancing:

Carmellia was all but inviting him to make love to her. He was embarrassed yet at the same time flattered because, without doubt, there was not another man in the room who would not willingly have changed places with him. Her scent – needless to say, that of camellias – was so strong it was almost overpowering.

By the time the dance came to an end, Carmellia had her cheek as well as her body pressed as close as was possible against him and she was humming the chorus softly in her husky voice: 'I'm crazy for you.'

Carmellia was making it plain she wanted to have sex with him, and he realized that had he not been in love with Toni, he might well have responded to this exotic woman's blatant advances. As it was, when she drew away reluctantly from his embrace and invited him and Toni to join her at her table, he was in two minds whether he wished to do so or not.

It was Toni who made up his mind. He left Carmellia, saying he would pass on the invitation to his wife. When he did so, Toni did not hesitate in replying emphatically in a cold voice that she did not wish to spend the rest of the evening with the film star.

'I'm no prude, as you know, Justin,' she said, 'but the way she was throwing herself at you – well, it was completely over the top – and I am certainly not going to be left sitting like that poor boy at her table whilst she seduces you on the dance floor.'

Her cheeks were flushed and she was breathing deeply in an effort to hide her distress. This, after all, was supposed to be their honeymoon. It was not yet forty-eight hours since they had arrived and now Justin was flirting with another woman.

He was frowning as he sat down beside her. 'There's no need to be like that, hon,' he said. 'You're not jealous, are you? I just thought it might be amusing! Come on, Toni, don't be a spoil-sport. Besides, it would look rude to refuse an invitation from someone as famous as she is!'

'Rude or not, I'm not going to spend the rest of the evening watching her ogling you – and if that's being jealous or rude, I don't care. You go and sit with her if you're so keen, but I'm *not* going.'

Piqued by Toni's unwillingness to do as he wanted, Justin tried another tack.

'Look, hon, you might find it interesting. I mean, she is quite a character, isn't she? And she's obviously bored with that miserable blond boy she's with, and . . .'

'And I'm not going!' Toni interrupted. 'You can go if you want, Justin. I'm going to bed!' She reached for her handbag and stood up, her movements so abrupt that she jarred the table in front of them, and Justin's half-finished glass of brandy toppled over. He started mopping it up as best he could with the paper napkins, his eyes angry.

'Just because you're in a temper, there's no need to be like that. For goodness' sake, sit down; everyone is staring at you.'

Making no move to do so, Toni stood glowering at him, her voice perilously near to tears as she said, 'Makes a change for them then, from staring at that . . . that woman flirting with you on the dance floor. As for your admirer, you can tell her I'm tired after the golf and am going to bed, and to disappoint anyone expecting us to have a row . . .' She broke off to reach up and kiss his cheek, saying in a loud voice: 'See you later, darling. Don't wake me if I'm asleep.'

Justin caught his breath. He was very angry, the more so as part of him thought that perhaps he should not have insisted they join Carmellia. In a way, Toni had a right to be jealous. He had not tried to put a little space between Carmellia's body and his as they had danced, and he most certainly would not have liked to watch Toni dancing and flirting with another man. On the other hand, she must have seen that it was Carmellia who was doing her best to seduce him, not the other way round. So much for her insistence that she would always trust him to be faithful to her.

To hell with it, he thought, beckoning the hovering waiter and ordering a bottle of champagne to be sent over to Carmellia's table. A look close to defiance now distorted his face as he stood up and walked purposefully across the dance floor to her table.

Upstairs in their beautiful big bedroom, Toni drew back the curtains, allowing the light of a full moon to flood the room. Tears were choking her as she undressed and climbed into bed. She was filled with conflicting emotions – appalled that they could be rowing on only the second day of their holiday, and ashamed of herself for walking out on the man she loved, who had been doing everything he could to make her happy. On the other hand, she had been horrified by the way he had been dancing with the film star – the same sexy way he usually held *her*. There was no denying that she was desperately jealous, but justifiably so! It was all Justin's fault for agreeing to dance with the woman, and leaving Toni alone at their table while no doubt everyone watching felt sorry for her.

SIX

Despite Toni's determination that Justin would find her asleep when he came to bed, she was still wide awake and increasingly miserable when, an hour later, he let himself into the room. She had left a light on in the sitting room but the bedroom was in darkness. She heard the clink of coins on the glass-topped table as he started to undress, and tried to keep her breathing unhurried. She heard him stumble once and wondered how much champagne he had drunk. At least, she thought, an hour was not long enough for the film star to have taken him to her bedroom.

When Justin moved into the bathroom and turned on the shower, Toni's unease increased. Would he believe she was asleep? What would be his mood? Would he be angry with her for not going to Carmellia's table and leaving in a huff? Had she the right to be angry that he was enjoying another woman's obvious adulation? Jealousy was a horrid thing. Perhaps *she* should apologise for spoiling their evening?

Despite her determination, tears trickled down her cheeks on to the pillow and she moved as close as she could to the edge of the huge double bed, knowing she would not be able to feign sleep if he touched her. The thought that they were actually so distanced from one another on this, only the second night of their holiday, was almost unbearable. Suppose they *had* got married, as they'd both wanted? Would she now be regretting it? Would she be fearful that, given sufficient temptation, Justin would be unfaithful to her? That she would never be able to trust him?

Her deliberations ceased abruptly as Justin closed the bathroom door and felt his way over to his side of the bed. Smelling strongly of toothpaste, he eased his way beneath the duvet and reached out his arm. Finding only empty space, he eased further over and his arm went round her. 'Are you asleep, hon?' he asked in a whisper.

Despite herself, her body stiffened and her breath came faster. She knew then that he guessed she was awake.

'Toni, darling, please don't turn away from me!' he said in a low, urgent tone. 'I'm sorry; I didn't mean to upset you! I never thought you might feel so strongly about . . . well, joining up with her – Carmellia. I mean, I suppose I thought you'd be interested in finding out more about her and the films she has made and . . .' He broke off, aware that Toni was crying. 'Please, darling, please don't be upset. I am sorry. I really am sorry that you were . . . well, hurt. I didn't think . . . I should have . . .'

Thoroughly undermined by his abject apologies, Toni now turned over and flung her arms round him, making no attempt to stem her tears. 'I'm the one who was silly!' she said. 'I just hated the way she was being so . . . so sexy . . . and with everyone watching . . . and you not seeming to mind . . . and then when you wanted us to go and sit at her table . . . and I was horribly jealous, and . . .'

Tears now choked her disjointed outburst, and she reached for a corner of the sheet in an attempt to wipe her eyes. Justin begged her not to cry and was planting desperate kisses on her mouth and cheeks. It was less than a minute before they were holding each other tight, and less time still before they were making love. This time, however, it was not the way they usually prolonged their pleasure in each other's bodies. It was almost a violent intent to be united again; to belong to each other again, to push the past few unhappy hours into oblivion.

When they finally fell asleep, exhausted, reassured, physically at peace, each believed the unhappy rift had now been relegated to the past. Lying curled on her side, Justin's body close against her back and his arms lying across her breast, Toni's last thought was that she had been both stupid and unfair to have refused the film star's invitation. It did not then cross her mind a second time, as it was to do later, that if an episode such as this had occurred once, there was no reason whatever why it could not happen again; that when the familiarity of married life had replaced the intensity of their new-found love, Justin might not be so certain to ignore the novelty of another woman's flattery and respond to another woman's desires.

*   *   *

When Toni awoke the next morning, Justin was no longer lying beside her. Opening her eyes, she saw him standing by the glass doors opening on to the balcony. His back was towards her and she was overcome by the desire to photograph him as he was at this moment: naked; his back, narrowing at the waist, ending in small, firm buttocks. His back and long, slim but muscular legs were tanned a beautiful golden brown. His fair hair curled into the nape of his neck and his arms were reaching up to either side of the doorway.

She felt an overwhelming desire to be standing behind him, her arms round his waist, her hands touching, holding him, feeling his growing need for her. Before she could do so, he turned and came across the room, smiling at her as he entered the bedroom and, leaning down, kissed her.

'You were sleeping so peacefully, I didn't want to wake you,' he said. 'It's such a lovely morning, I had to get up and I've been gazing at the sea – it's like a millpond – and that bald chap we saw yesterday is in the pool doing his fifty lengths again, poor guy!'

Laughing, he kissed her again and smoothed the hair back from her face. 'I love to see you like this – all rosy cheeked and sleepy. I do love you so much!' He kissed her again and smiled.

'I thought we might have breakfast on the balcony,' he said. 'Can't think when I last had a meal outside. What do you think? There's a room service menu on the desk and we can have almost anything we want, although there is not quite the same huge variety as downstairs. I'm ravenous! I know you don't like a cooked breakfast but as we are playing golf again this morning and may miss lunch, I hope you'll let me order a proper meal for you.'

It was a moment before Toni replied. She was far from sure if she was physically up to playing eighteen holes of golf after their late night. It must have been two o'clock before they had finally fallen asleep. However, she could not bring herself to veto Justin's enthusiastic plans. He really loved his golf, but the past winter had been so cold, wet and miserable that he'd had very little opportunity to play. Although there had not been much snow in London, the rain and cold wind had been continuous, and many of the outlying golf courses were waterlogged. Today, she reminded herself, they were playing again with the Stonehouses and would be going round the course in a buggy. At least Justin never got annoyed if she wasn't playing very well, she told herself with a smile. He was more concerned with his own game.

'To please you I'll have an omelette and bacon,' she said, 'and a croissant and butter and honey and a gallon of coffee. How does that sound?'

'Do you know something, my darling, I really, really love you!' Justin replied. 'If I wasn't so damned hungry, I'd suggest we skipped breakfast and made love instead.'

Toni laughed. 'If you want me to play golf, then you'd better put that idea on the back burner,' she said. 'And if we're booked for the same time as yesterday, you'd better order breakfast right now!'

Laughing happily, Justin went into the bathroom, took the two fluffy white towelling bathrobes off their hooks and carried them together with the his-and-hers matching slippers back into the bedroom. Donning his own bathrobe, he went back into the sitting room and rang for room service.

The meal, eaten in the beautiful warm sunshine on the balcony, was so enjoyable that they lingered there until the last minute. Toni was fascinated by the house martins building nests in any suitable place on the façade of the hotel. They darted to and fro, sometimes skimming the blue pool water which reflected on their undersides, causing them to appear to have turquoise feathers.

Justin was more interested in the shallow end of the swimming pool where about twenty elderly or middle-aged hotel guests were gathering for their morning exercise session. The instructor in immaculate white trousers and singlet stood on the poolside shouting instructions to them through a megaphone as if they were a class of schoolchildren. Justin was laughing. 'I imagine most of those wealthy guests spend ninety per cent of their lives giving orders,' he said, 'yet there they are obeying orders, presumably in the hope of improving their health, or figures!'

'Don't be so critical!' Toni reproached him. 'One day you may be as old and fat as they are and unable to take more strenuous exercise.'

Watching him two hours later as he reached his arms above his head to drive his ball almost the length of the fairway, she thought how sad it was that someone with such a beautiful, athletic body like Justin's must inevitably descend into decrepitude. When they themselves were in their sixties, seventies, eighties, would they still come to this beautiful hotel and try to improve their health in the big swimming pool?

Justin now took her driver out of her golf bag and handed it to her, saying, 'It's a good idea to keep your mind on the game, hon! Bet if my ball is lost, you wouldn't know where to start looking for it!'

Obediently, Toni took up her position on the ladies' tee and, without a practice swing, hit the ball as far as she could. Beside her, Justin let out a whistle of approval and gave her a congratulatory kiss as she climbed back into the buggy beside him. It was a lucky shot but she had no intention of telling him so.

Both they and the Stonehouses played well – particularly Justin – until they reached the seventeenth hole. On one side of the fairway was a small lake with a steep bank leading down to the water's edge. Justin drove his usual lengthy distance but this time his ball did not go straight. He found it lodged in the side of the bank and frowned. 'Not going to be easy to get out of here!' he exclaimed.

'Why not pick the ball up and drop it on the fairway?' Toni suggested. 'We're only one hole down.'

'Because if I pick it up I'll lose a stroke!' Justin replied as he tried to juggle himself into a safe position. 'And I don't intend to let them go two up!'

'We're only playing a friendly, not a competition!' Toni said as she and the Stonehouses from the other side of the fairway watched Justin trying desperately to find a suitable foothold from which to strike his ball.

He lifted his club to chop at his ball a second time and his foot slipped. He fell forward against the bank, swearing as he saw his ball now freed and sliding down into the water. He did not get up instantly, and Toni hurried down to him to lend assistance. One leg was twisted under him, and although he insisted that he was perfectly able to get out by himself, he was in fact humiliatingly unable to do so.

Toni leaned forward and handed her club to him. He grasped it but despite his renewed efforts he still could not extricate his leg from beneath him.

She turned to wave to Peter Stonehouse to come and help, but he was already on his way. With his assistance, Justin was hauled back up on to the fairway where he sat, on the passenger seat of the buggy, his face distorted with pain.

''Fraid I've fucked up my ankle!' he gasped. Justin so seldom swore – at least not in front of her – that Toni knew the injury must be pretty bad. Gemma had now joined them and was gently pulling down Justin's knee-length golf sock. He caught his breath.

'Swelling a bit already!' she said sympathetically. 'Guess you're going to have to call it a day.'

Justin bit his lip, wincing as he touched his foot. He looked up at Toni. 'Think you'll have to drive me back to the clubhouse. I'll get some cold water there to put on this wretched thing.' He looked at the Stonehouses. 'I'm so sorry – I ruined our game. Toni was quite right: I shouldn't have been so stubborn insisting on playing the bloody ball from down there.'

He broke off and she saw him wincing as Peter tried to move his injured leg into the buggy.

'You two finish your game,' Toni said. 'I'll drive him to the hospital in Malaga. There must be one there. We can get him X-rayed to make sure nothing is broken.'

Despite the Stonehouses' offer to accompany them, both Justin and Toni insisted they could cope on their own.

Two hours later, Justin was lying white-faced in a private room in Hospital Carlos Haya in Malaga, where he had been given painkillers whilst awaiting an X-ray.

There had been a particularly nasty road accident not half an hour before Justin had been admitted, and as he was not an emergency, he'd been told he would have to wait before he could receive attention. Meanwhile, a nurse had taken a preliminary look at his leg, pronounced the possibility of a broken ankle and switched on a television set to divert him while he waited.

'I feel like such a bloody idiot!' he said. 'If it is broken I may have to have crutches until the swelling has gone down and they'll put the ruddy ankle in plaster. I've ruined our holiday and . . .'

His voice broke and he stopped talking as Toni said gently, 'It was an accident, darling. Could have happened to anyone. It's just bad luck, and you haven't ruined my holiday. We'll find lots of ways to enjoy ourselves without golf and skiing.'

She could see he was still in pain, and the pain relief they had given him was making him drowsy.

The television set in the corner of the room was now showing a football match. Toni turned up the sound and, although the commentary was in Spanish, Justin's depression was diverted.

'Mind if I watch?' he asked.

Smiling, Toni shook her head. 'I left my Kindle in the car; I'll go fetch it so I can carry on reading my book. I've got the car keys.'

Justin was now engrossed in the game and she hurried down in the lift and out to the car park. It was even more crowded than before and, as she made her way back to the vast hospital, she became slightly disorientated. Realizing as she went into the building that she had entered by a different doorway from the one they'd used on their arrival, she looked for a sign indicating the lifts. They, too, were crowded, and a stout Spanish woman was blocking the floor number indicator. Without looking at Toni, she pressed her plump white finger on one of the buttons and the lift shot up, stopping for the first time on the third floor, where she got out. Following after her, Toni realized at once that the corridor was not the one where the hospital orderly had wheeled Justin's chair to the assessment room.

Thoroughly disorientated, she looked for a sign indicating which way she should go, but could only see one saying EXIT. Whilst she was wondering whether to wait for a lift to take her back down to the ground floor, a hospital orderly came along the passage wheeling an empty trolley. Toni tried to explain that she was looking for the place where casualties waited for attention, but he replied apologetically in Spanish that he did not speak English. With a last hope of making her needs understood, Toni tried to indicate Justin's injury by simulating his fall and pointing to her foot. The blank expression on the man's face gave way to one of comprehension.

'*Si, si, Señora! Accidente!*' Smiling, he pointed down the corridor, past the EXIT sign and, holding up three fingers of one hand, pointed with his other arm to the left.

Toni was far from sure if these directions to take the third left turn were correct, but as the orderly disappeared down the corridor, she followed his directions and went the other way. By

the time she came to the third left turn, she was in no doubt that
she was nowhere near the waiting room where Justin had been
taken. She was, she thought, almost certainly on the wrong floor.

Whilst still pondering what she should now do, a doctor in a
white coat emerged from one of the closed doors in front of her.
He looked to be in a hurry but Toni quickly grabbed his arm and
explained that she was searching for a recently admitted casualty.
'An Englishman . . . *Inglés*,' she added in Spanish.

The doctor regarded her with a look of surprise. 'Your husband
did not tell me he was expecting a visitor,' he said in heavily
accented but otherwise faultless English. 'He is very depressed
so I am delighted to see you.' He used the words carefully,
having been advised that the wife of his patient, the unfortunate
Englishman who had been paralysed in a fall in the Sierra
Nevada, had died from her injuries. This pretty young woman
was not, therefore, his wife.

It took several more minutes for Toni to explain how and why
she happened to be where she was, and that she knew nothing
about his patient.

'I will redirect you to the department you are seeking, *Señora*,'
he said, 'but I have a small duty to perform first. It will take me
only five minutes. Do you have time to wait for me?'

Toni nodded. 'That is very kind of you, Doctor. I'm in no
hurry at all, so I'll be happy to wait for you. I don't fancy getting
lost again.'

For a moment, he did not speak, but then did so in a hesitant
voice. 'Would you be so very kind as to spend a few minutes with
my patient? He is English and he speaks no Spanish so has no
one to talk to. It is certain now that he has broken his neck. He
cannot move and we cannot advise his family as he tells us he has
no relations, only those of his wife who live in India. He is very
badly injured and he needs a relative or friend to support him at
this time, but will not give us a name of who we might contact.'

Shocked by the unfortunate man's plight, Toni asked: 'Is he
. . . Will he . . .?'

'Die?' the doctor said, anticipating her question. 'It is possible
but we cannot be certain yet until we have more pictures.
Tomorrow he will have another scan, and we shall know more.
Now, if you are quite happy to visit my patient . . .?'

When Toni nodded, he opened the door and led her over to the bedside of a young man strapped to a board so that he was immobilized. His hair was brown with a hint of red; his eyes, which were open, were a surprising clear grey fringed with very dark lashes. Superficial cuts on his face, arms and hands were painted in patches of a coloured antiseptic; other parts were bandaged. Despite all his many injuries, he was still a good-looking man. The doctor excused himself and hurried away, leaving Toni on the chair beside the bed. In as calm a voice as she could manage, she introduced herself and asked him his name.

The patient's eyes fastened on her and his heavily swollen lips moved as he said in a hoarse whisper: 'Aaron – Aaron Osborn.'

Toni's heart filled with pity. It was obvious to her that even talking was an effort, although he managed to say how good it was to have an English-speaking visitor. She explained how she came to be there, that she had got lost on her way back to her injured partner and the doctor had asked her to pop by for a few minutes before he took her to find Justin. There was barely time to tell him about the fabulous Hotel Los Palmeros before the doctor returned to the room.

'The nurse is on her way with your medicines,' he said to Aaron. 'I'll be back to see you tomorrow morning. I must take your visitor away now. Perhaps she will be able to visit you again another time.'

Toni was about to protest that, sorry as she was for the unfortunate man, she could not possibly become a regular visitor. Then she realized that Justin would almost certainly be returning to the hospital for further treatment to his ankle. Smiling at Aaron, she told him she would visit him again in a day or two when Justin returned for a check-up. Although the paralysed man did not speak as she got up to go, she was aware of his unusual grey eyes fastened on her, and for some strange reason she felt herself blushing as she left the room.

SEVEN

J ustin was allowed to leave the hospital, the X-rays having shown that there were no bones broken; it was just a very severe sprain. He must not walk on it, he was told, which, he said miserably to Toni, meant no more golf, no water skiing, no dancing, no exercise of any sort for at least a week, maybe more.

Toni managed to hide her disappointment, telling herself that at least Justin did not have the prolonged restrictions of a broken bone. As she drove him back to the hotel, a pair of crutches lent by the hospital on the back seat, she did her best to console him.

'The medics didn't say anything about not making love!' she said with a smile. 'Anyway, I'd just as soon be lazy and sunbathe by the pool.'

Justin's miserable expression remained unchanged as he said, 'I only hope I'll be mobile again before we go home.'

Toni was aware of his plans to join his three best friends for a ten-day golfing holiday in the States on their return home. It was, he'd told her, an annual event the four of them had enjoyed since their university days. All three were from the north of England and Toni had not met them.

'All the more reason to do what the medics say if you want to go on your golfing holiday,' Toni said. 'I know you, Justin – you'll want to try out your ankle every day and end up making things worse.'

The next eleven days were not as ecstatic as the first three had been. Justin did his best to hide his frustration, but he quickly became bored lounging by the pool. The Stonehouses came up from their bungalow to spend an hour or so talking to him but, nice as they were, he quickly became bored by the lack of physical activity.

He found some amusement watching the extraordinary assort-ment of sun-worshippers who, oiled and stripped to as near nakedness as possible, lay motionless on their sun loungers for hours on end. Very occasionally, one would get up and dive into the pool and, more entertainingly, one or two girls in barely visible bikinis would sashay round the edge showing off their slim, tanned bodies. From time to time, one such female would turn her head and stare openly at his athletic body, now beautifully bronzed and, ignoring Toni, give him a flirtatious smile.

At least the glamorous Carmellia del Concordia had left the hotel before making an appearance by the pool. It was one thing, Toni told herself, to have such an exceptionally good-looking boyfriend, but she would have to accustom herself to the fact that other women also found Justin extremely attractive and that, understandably, he could not fail to be flattered by the obvious admiration he evoked in the opposite sex.

Jealousy was an aspect of their relationship that she had not previously experienced during the four short months they had been together. At their first meeting, she had fallen head over heels in love with him and been proud that her friends were all in awe of him. He was tall, good looking, amusing, the right age and, not least, rich! To those adjectives, she could have added that he was a wonderful lover. Every spare moment when she was not at work and he had no engagement elsewhere they had spent in his or her flat. Within six weeks they had known they wished to spend the rest of their lives together and Justin had proposed.

'Six weeks is not long enough to know if that is the right decision,' her boss, Julia, a charming, friendly woman, had warned. 'Marriage is – or should be – a lifetime commitment. Get to know him a bit better, Toni, and then make up your mind.'

There was no need to get married so quickly, her best friend, Chrissie, had said when Toni told her Justin wanted them to get married immediately. It wasn't as if she was pregnant! And even if she were, lots of couples these days didn't bother about marriage. Justin, however, was really anxious for them to tie the knot. 'I want to know you're mine, not just for now but for ever!' he'd declared passionately. 'If you are my wife, other guys won't come after you. You're such an innocent, babe! You don't know how attractive you are!'

As far as she herself was concerned, Toni only knew that for the first time in her life she had fallen in love – properly in love

– and that Justin was the man she had so often imagined spending the rest of her life with.

Watching Justin wave a cheerful goodbye to one of the girls who had been flirting with him, Toni told herself sharply that she must now take a hold on herself and stop being so possessive. What possible harm was there in a man, a husband, a lover, finding other women amusing, sexually attractive, so long as it did not become a relationship? Quite probably all young men noticed a pretty, sexy girl, but were not so obvious about it as Justin. He had openly ogled Carmellia, but so had every other male within sight. It did not mean he loved Toni any less, or that he now found his two pretty admirers more attractive than he found her. She was being paranoid to doubt him – to imagine it had the slightest detrimental effect upon their relationship.

The remaining ten days of their holiday were as near idyllic as was possible with the restrictions on their activities. Justin's injury did not affect the closeness of their lovemaking nor their pleasure in each other's company. Two days before the holiday came to an end, Justin's ankle had returned to its rightful size and he was able to discard his hated crutches. He could, he maintained, return to the golf course, and perhaps even try a water-skiing session before they went home.

Toni insisted that he must take medical advice first. Reminding him of his forthcoming golf holiday in the States, she managed to persuade him to let her drive him into Malaga to see his doctor immediately after breakfast, pointing out that they would be back at the hotel long before lunch, which would still allow them to get down to the beach and book a water-skiing session.

It was a beautiful morning with only a slight breeze, the sea as calm as a mill pond as they set off along the coast road to Malaga. Justin was now in excellent spirits and spent most of the short journey telling Toni what an absolute brick she had been about the whole unfortunate disruption to their plans. Not once, he said, had she reminded him that it was entirely his stubborn fault that caused the injury, and he wanted her to know that he loved her all the more because of her unselfishness and the trouble she had taken to keep his depression at bay.

The Stonehouses had been frequent companions and quite often dined with them at night. The four of them got on so well that they had agreed to go to the Stonehouses' favourite fish restaurant for their last evening in Spain.

Justin's subsequent good humour was, however, sorely tried when they reached the hospital and were told that the consultant he had come to see would be detained for a further half hour, and he was requested to wait. He was all for giving up the visit, which he had thought unnecessary anyway, and returning to the hotel.

'We might even be able to book a round of golf if we skip lunch,' he said. Toni, however, thought the risk too great, and reminded him that he only had, quite literally, to put one foot wrong to ruin his forthcoming holiday in America.

The consultant's waiting room was cool and comfortable. His receptionist brought them coffee and Justin found a magazine about underwater exploration, a subject in which he had recently become interested. A doctor came into the room in search of a lost patient, and Toni recognized him as the *médico* who had assisted her when she was lost and had taken her to visit the Englishman with the broken back. She enquired how he was getting on.

'Physically he is doing quite well,' he told her, 'but he is still very depressed. I have not seen him smile since I spoke to him of your visit. It is sad that the poor young man has no relatives or friends in Spain to visit him and raise his spirits.'

Toni turned to Justin. 'As you have to wait half an hour – and here in Spain that almost certainly means twice as long – I'll go and put my head round the door of the patient's room. Maybe there is someone – a relative or friend in England who I could contact for him – who could come out here for a while. It must be pretty grim being on your own when you have to face the fact that not only has your wife died, but you could even be paralysed for the rest of your life.'

When she entered Aaron's room five minutes later, the unfortunate invalid stared at her from his bed with a desperate look in his eyes.

Toni sat down on the chair beside the bed and said gently, 'Do you remember me? I came in to visit you last week. My name is Antonia Ward. I'm here on holiday with my boyfriend, who damaged his ankle on the golf course. I left him downstairs waiting for the doctor to arrive and discharge him. Is there anything at all I can do for you?'

He shook his head but did not speak.

'The first time I saw you they told me you had been skiing with your wife when the accident happened. I don't suppose you do remember me,' she said.

At mention of his wife, the man's eyes closed momentarily and Toni felt desperately sorry that she had mentioned the accident which, the nurse had told her previously, had caused his wife to fall hundreds of metres down the mountainside.

Aaron's eyes opened and he stared at her silently for a moment before saying, 'I'd rather not talk about it, but thank you for coming to see me.'

He then proceeded to tell her in a desperate rush of words that his surgeon had operated on his neck. He had done a bone graft on one of the vertebrae and fitted a metal plate. He had then been immobilized by a plaster cast and been told he must remain in it for a minimum of six weeks – possibly twelve – when hopefully he might regain movement in his body. He was, he said, in considerable pain as well as discomfort from the severe bruising he had sustained, but he was, according to his surgeon, extremely lucky not to have broken his spine further down, which would definitely have paralysed him.

His somewhat unusual grey eyes filled with tears. 'My orthopaedic consultant said that, as I am insured, I can be flown back to England in due course and I imagine I can be sent to Stoke Mandeville Hospital in Buckinghamshire, which I believe copes with wrecks like me.' His eyes sought Toni's as he added weakly: 'Can't even wipe my own eyes!'

Her heart aching with pity, Toni found a box of tissues by the bedside and wiped the tears on his cheeks.

'I saw a programme about Stoke Mandeville a week or two before we came on holiday,' she said gently. 'It was about soldiers returning from Afghanistan and the miracles they can perform at that hospital. I'm sure you'll have a total recovery if you do what you are told,' she added, smiling.

He did not return her smile. 'Did the doc tell you about the accident?' he asked abruptly. Without waiting for her reply, he said in a harsh, expressionless voice, 'We – my wife, Leena, and I – had gone out to a Sierra Nevada skiing resort an hour or so away from here. We and two friends had booked a chalet for ten days' skiing. At the last minute, one of them developed appendicitis and they called off the trip, leaving my wife and me to go on our own. The snow was quite good and on the first two days we did fairly easy red runs to get our muscles going, then decided to tackle one of the black runs the next day. There was a hard frost that night, but although we knew it would be a bit icy, we're both experienced skiers, so . . .'

He stopped suddenly and asked Toni: 'Would you rather I didn't tell you this? It's just that you're the first English person I've seen since I've been *compos mentis* who understands what I've been trying to explain.'

He was dry-eyed now and, encouraged by Toni to continue, he went on in a carefully controlled voice. 'Leena was leading the way. The sun was shining but there weren't all that many skiers around because of the icy patches on the run where it was shaded by trees. Leena was going too fast, I realized, as we approached a particularly narrow part of the path where it crossed the mountainside. The traverse was risky in places because of the steep drop on the right-hand side, and there was plastic netting and signs to show it was quite dangerous. I was told that the drop was hundreds of feet or more over rocks sticking up above the snow, so I called to Leena to slow down, but . . .'

He broke off to look up at Toni, willing her to listen as he said huskily: 'She slipped on one of the particularly icy bends. Her skis slid sideways and she crashed through the netting and over the edge . . .' He broke off to clear his throat and then said, 'She disappeared! I managed to stop myself and climbed back, praying she had not fallen too far. Stupidly, I suppose – I was still wearing my skis – I leaned over the edge of the path and, next thing I knew, I was hurtling down. I heard one of my legs snap and then . . . then . . . I must have hit a rock. I don't remember anything more but they told me when I regained my senses that I'd been lucky to fall where I did; that an outcrop of rocks had prevented me falling hundreds of feet further down into the crevasse below.'

He paused for a few seconds and then, in a carefully controlled voice, he said, 'I was told the mountain rescue team managed to get me down in the blood wagon strapped to a board and that a helicopter rushed me here. I was unconscious, of course, so I couldn't tell them about Leena, and it was three days before a party of mountain climbers found her. She'd fallen hundreds of feet further down than I had . . .' He broke off, his eyes closed once more as if to shut out the memory.

Toni took a deep breath. 'I'm so very sorry!' she said gently, and although she was unsure if his hand had any feeling, she covered it with her own. 'Have they located your parents yet? Are they on their way to be with you?'

Aaron, lying motionless in the bed, opened his eyes once more to look at her. 'My parents are dead. I was brought up by an uncle. He died last year,' he said flatly.

Toni stole a quick glance at her watch and saw that she had left Justin over twenty minutes ago and ought now to say a quick goodbye to the patient, but she was filled with pity for him, lying there paralysed. The fact that he had told her, a complete stranger, about all these unhappy, tragic events in his life, somehow made her feel obliged to help him if there was any way in which she could do so. It must be so awful to be alone in a foreign country, unable to move or to know what your future would be.

'Your wife's family . . .' she said tentatively. 'Will they—?'

'No!' he broke in. 'They are Indian, not English. They came to Spain to attend their daughter's cremation, and visited me once to ask for my permission to have Leena's ashes flown back to India before returning home. I think they have a twisted idea that I was responsible for their daughter's death in some way; that I should not have allowed her to ski that black run knowing it was dangerous even in good conditions. I've been lying here wondering if perhaps they are right, but . . .'

He broke off, giving a long, drawn-out sigh, which sounded filled with pain.

'I am so sorry you've been having such a dreadful time,' she said. 'I suppose the one consolation is that you broke your neck and not your back – otherwise you certainly would have been paralysed. Things will get better – they must do, because they can't get much worse,' she added with a smile as she stood up to go. 'I'm afraid I won't be able to visit you again because we fly home the day after tomorrow, but if there is anything I can do for you back in England . . .?'

Seeing his downcast expression, she added: 'Look, I'll give you my email address so you can contact me when you return. If you'd like me to, I'll try to visit you at Stoke Mandeville – that is, if you end up there, although I'm sure all your friends will rally round you once they hear your sad news. I really must go now or Justin, my boyfriend, will think I'm lost and start a search of the hospital for me.'

A look of acute bitterness distorted Aaron's face as he said, 'Lucky guy, your boyfriend, having a woman like you to bother about him!'

Overcome with pity, Toni gave his hand a gentle squeeze. 'I'm sure you will be back on your feet again before too long,' she said. 'And I shall expect you to contact me and let me know when that happens. I'll be crossing my fingers!'

When she stood up to go, she was conscious once again of his strange, sad grey eyes following her as she left the room.

EIGHT

'Where in God's name have you been?'

Justin's tone of voice was unlike any he had used with Toni before. He had risen to his feet from one of the chairs in the waiting room and his eyes were as stormy as his voice.

'I'm sorry you had to wait for me,' Toni said. 'I stayed longer than I had intended. What news about your ankle?'

Ignoring her question, he asked her a second time what had kept her. 'You said you were just going to put your head round the door to see how the man was.'

'I said I was sorry!' Toni replied. 'And I wish you wouldn't speak to me like that, Justin. I stayed longer then I had intended as Aaron was very depressed and I tried to cheer him up a bit. You wouldn't like it if you were stuck in a hospital in a foreign country unable to move and with no relatives or friends to support you!'

Justin's tone softened and his expression returned to normal. 'Sorry I shouted at you, hon. I was getting worried when you didn't come back. I suppose the medic gave me an all clear more quickly than I'd expected, so I've been waiting here for you, watching the clock and not knowing where the hell you were. I'd begun to worry that you'd got lost again or had an accident or something. None of the nurses I asked seemed to understand who I was talking about when I said you were visiting a paralysed Englishman.'

He crossed the room and reached out his arm, intending to put it round her, but despite his apology, Toni was not yet ready for the intimacy. The feeling of shock at his words and his tone of voice when she entered the room was as unfamiliar as it was unwelcome. However worried Justin had been, he had no right to address her in that way; she was, after all, supposed to be his girlfriend, the girl he intended to marry.

With an effort, Toni managed to put such thoughts aside. She had not meant to stay so long with the bedridden man, but as if his physical state was not awful enough, he had also lost his wife in the same skiing accident.

'You know, Justin, you would have been as desperate as he was to see a friendly face and be able to converse with someone other than a foreigner or a member of the hospital staff if you'd been in Aaron's position,' she said. 'I don't see why you should begrudge him ten minutes of my time.'

Justin looked sheepish as he stared down at Toni's flushed cheeks. 'I'm not denying that the poor guy must have been hellishly pleased to see you, but you can't go round the world giving your time and sympathy to every Tom, Dick and Harry who wants it. I suppose I was a bit put out that you'd forgotten I could be waiting for you.' Once more he put out his arm and, this time, was able to draw her to him. 'I thought something nasty must have happened to you – you'd got trapped in a lift or fallen down some stairs or something!' He tried a tentative smile.

Toni relaxed against him. 'I'm sorry, too,' she said softly. 'Well, now you've been given the all clear, there won't be a next time for me to visit the poor man.'

The last thing either of them expected as they drove back to the hotel was that less than forty-eight hours later, Toni would return to the hospital, this time as a patient herself.

On the last night before Toni and Justin were due to fly home, their new friends, Peter and Gemma Stonehouse, insisted upon taking them to their favourite fish restaurant.

Ever since the upset at the hospital, Justin had insisted that they made up for lost time. The temperature had risen into the high twenties and he had immediately arranged for them to enjoy all the sporting activities he knew she loved, and he was his most loving self both in and out of bed. Toni knew she should welcome such attentions but she could not forget the tone of recrimination in his voice at the hospital. It was a facet of Justin's temperament she had not come across before. Would there be other occasions in the future, she asked herself, when he would speak to her like that?

She now encountered another aspect of Justin's character which had been unknown to her prior to this holiday. She wished suddenly that they were not eating out with the Stonehouses, but Justin was really keen to join the couple and eat somewhere other than the hotel restaurant.

When she suggested she might prefer an intimate evening alone with him, he had sulked like a small boy about to be deprived of his pocket money. As they changed for the evening, she found herself wondering quite frighteningly if her parents might be right – that she and Justin had not known each other long enough to be certain that they were really suited to be married; that there might be other sides to Justin that she had yet to discover. However, when he pointed out that an hour before they were due to join the Stonehouses was far too late to call off the evening, she realized she was being extremely unreasonable and admitted it to him.

Much later, after a very pleasant evening with the Stonehouses, as she was lying in the big hotel bed in Justin's arms making love, she wondered how she could ever have doubted their suitability to marry. They had had a really fun evening, the four of them exchanging jokes and stories, enjoying a superb meal of freshly cooked seafood and promising to visit one another in England in the summer. She had, Toni told herself, been extremely childish, over-possessive and selfish in her wish to keep Justin entirely to herself. She loved his gregarious nature; loved the fact that he made friends so easily, and that he was popular with everyone he met, both men and women. Before she fell asleep, she made a promise to herself to ensure that the next day – their last – would be as perfect for Justin as she could possibly make it.

Her promise proved to be impossible to keep. They had not been asleep more than four hours when she woke up with acute stomach pains and nausea. Her subsequent visit to the bathroom was one of the worst – the most painful – she had ever experienced. The spasms of pain were so bad that her gasps woke Justin. He found her doubled up in agony and, realizing there was nothing he could do to help her, he rang the night porter to ask him to get a doctor. When the man finally understood that it was a serious medical emergency, he said he would telephone the local *médico* who was available at all times for the hotel guests, although his charges for a visit after midnight were very high.

Assured that Justin was more than prepared to meet any costs, the porter rang the doctor's emergency number and was able to inform Justin that the *médico* would be at the hotel within twenty minutes.

When Justin returned to the bathroom, Toni was still vomiting and was only semi-conscious. Her temperature seemed to be vacillating between extremes of hot and cold and she was still doubled up with pain. Her eyes closed in relief when Justin told her a doctor was on his way. When he did arrive, it did not take him long to diagnose acute food poisoning – obviously as a result of something she had eaten in the fish restaurant. He then stressed that, because of the amount of fluids Toni had been and was still losing, she needed to go to hospital where she could be put on a drip before she became seriously dehydrated.

Justin regarded the doctor in dismay. He and Toni were due to fly home that evening, he explained. Their tickets were not exchangeable. The doctor shook his head. Food poisoning could be a serious matter, he said, and if his diagnosis was correct, it could be two or three days before the *señora* was well enough to travel.

Tests would have to be taken and her temperature returned to normal, the doctor told him. At the moment it was extremely high and he suspected this was no minor attack of food poisoning. He used his mobile phone to summon an ambulance.

Justin went over to the bedside where Toni now lay exhausted beneath a covering of bath towels, her head on one of the pillows, also covered with a towel. The doctor had given her some medication but it was far too soon for it to have helped with the pain.

'I'll go and get dressed so I'll be ready to go to the hospital with you, darling,' he said. 'I'll follow in the car so I can drive on to the airport to see if I can get our departure date postponed.'

In a voice that was both weak and unsteady, Toni said, 'You can't postpone your flight home, Justin. Have you forgotten you're flying to America three days after tomorrow?'

Justin's expression became one of dismay. 'Oh God, yes!' After a minute, he added, 'But I can't go and leave you here on your own.'

'I can manage!' Toni said weakly. 'I don't expect they'll keep me in hospital for more than a day or two, and I'm quite capable of flying home on my own.'

Justin's expression became thoughtful. 'Are you sure, hon? I really don't like the idea of leaving you ill like this. I could give Matt a buzz and tell him to try to find someone to replace me to make up the four?' He looked doubtful as he added, 'I don't suppose BA would let anyone else use my ticket to New York, but I could offer to pay for it, I suppose.'

Toni's eyes filled with tears. She felt so ill – ill enough to be glad the doctor was insisting on her going to hospital to be put on a drip. She was still gripped by spasmodic, agonizing pains, and her whole body seemed to ache from her constant vomiting.

Two hours later, lying in a hospital bed attached to a drip, she felt both weak and tearful. Whilst the preliminaries of her admission were taking place, Justin had taken the opportunity to drive to Malaga Airport to see if he could get the departure date of their tickets exchanged. She was not surprised when he returned with the news that they were not exchangeable.

'You must use yours, Justin!' she told him. 'Honestly, there's nothing you can do here and you can't let the three other guys down. I promise I'll be all right.'

When he still looked doubtful, she added: 'I'm sure I'll soon be feeling much better and your flight doesn't leave until this evening so you can get packed this afternoon and come and see me before you go.'

Although Justin still sounded uncertain, she detected a faint look of relief on his face. The boys' golf foursome in the States had been planned after a similar holiday the year before, and dates and plane bookings had been made a long time ago. He'd talked about it many times, and she was in no doubt how much he was looking forward to it.

Justin stayed by Toni's bedside until her pain diminished, then left to return to the hotel to clear the room which they were supposed to vacate by midday. He would get one of the maids to pack Toni's belongings in her suitcase, he said, which he would leave with the hall porter. He also intended to ask the Stonehouses if they would be kind enough to bring the case to Toni and see her safely to the airport when her flight was rebooked. When he kissed her goodbye, he looked a lot happier having made these arrangements, and it was obvious to Toni that he was feeling a lot less guilty about leaving her.

She woke an hour later when a nurse arrived to fix up a fresh bottle of fluid and give her some medication and a welcome cup of weak tea. She was in a lot less pain, but still nauseous. The sympathetic nurse took her to the bathroom and then settled her once more in her bed. Left alone when the nurse departed, Toni began to feel distressed about Justin's plans. She knew that, had it been Justin lying in a hospital bed, there was no way she would have left him to recover alone abroad and flown home on her own, even if he encouraged her to do so. She would have cancelled any of her own plans rather than let him be alone. Then quickly she reprimanded herself for such a thought. He had three friends depending on his company and she would be perfectly well able to travel on her own.

Nevertheless, tears dripped down her cheeks from beneath her closed eyelids. She tried to tell herself that women were different from men; they were by instinct carers. Men were not as sensitive to the feelings of others. It was not as if she was dangerously ill; lots of people got food poisoning when they were abroad – not, perhaps, if they ate in five-star restaurants like the one in the Hotel Los Palmeros, but in small restaurants such as the one to which Gemma and Peter had taken them. She had been the only one of the four to eat the scallops, one of which must so unluckily have been contaminated.

When Toni awoke from another light sleep, it was to be presented with a letter from Justin scribbled on hotel writing paper. Delivered by Peter Stonehouse, who had been shopping in Malaga, it read that Justin had managed to pack everything, had settled their hotel bill and instructed the hall porter to look after her suitcase until either she or one of the Stonehouses collected it. He had spoken to Gemma, who would be in to see her in the morning. Justin himself should be with her by four o'clock that afternoon.

When he arrived, after enquiring about her recovery, his mood was far more cheerful, even a little boastful as he recounted that he had thought of everything, even to give Peter Stonehouse some money to pay the hospital bill and to cover the cost of her ticket home. He had also telephoned Toni's mother to explain why her daughter's return would be delayed, but assured her that Toni was in no danger and would let her parents know when she had booked a flight.

Toni did her utmost to sound as cheerful as he did. It was obvious to her that his earlier qualms about going home without her had completely vanished. His mood was that of a young son whose mother had praised him for being such a good, thoughtful boy.

He left quite early, not only because he had to check-in for his flight, but he also had to return their hired car first.

Mercifully, Toni was given a sleeping pill that night so her depression did not keep her awake. She woke in the morning only because the nurse arrived with the doctor.

His visit was happily reassuring. She was no longer in pain and, if her tests proved she was no longer dehydrated, she could come off the drip. If all continued to go well she would be strong enough to travel home in a day or two.

Toni's eyes filled with tears as the doctor left the room. She knew it was ridiculous, but if she could not go home sooner, she would not be able to see Justin before he departed for the States, and then she would not see him for three whole weeks. He should never have left her alone here in hospital in Spain . . .

Knowing she was being unfair and that she herself had told him to go home without her, she made an effort to pull herself together. When Gemma Stonehouse arrived a while later, Toni was dry-eyed and able to greet her new friend with a smile.

'What a nice surprise!' she said, indicating a chair by the window where her visitor could be seated. 'I wasn't expecting to see you so soon.'

Gemma's homely face broke into a smile. 'Your better half told us you were a bit down in the dumps!' she said. 'Besides which, I thought you would almost certainly be needing these . . .'

She put a carrier bag on the bed containing a nightie and some toiletries, as well as Toni's make-up case, including her brush and comb.

'Justin hadn't a clue what you might want!' she said, laughing. 'The poor guy was in quite a state – said you usually did the packing, folded things and so on. I thought the days of helpless males had long since gone, although I have to say, Peter also seems to think I should do all the packing!' She laughed. 'Justin was in such a state by the time he rang for the porter to collect the luggage, he nearly walked out of the room leaving both of your passports in the safe!'

She looked at Toni's pale face and said sympathetically, 'What bad luck the pair of you have been having! First Justin's ankle and now you . . .'

She broke off as a nurse came into the room carrying a beautiful bunch of white roses, which she handed to Toni. 'From the English *señor* in *camera quinientos cuatro*,' she said, smiling broadly. 'He ask me to buy for you and give you this. I write for him so he ask for the *señora* please to *perdona*!'

Gemma was smiling as she watched the nurse leave the room to find a vase. 'Don't tell me you have a secret admirer!' she said. 'Is it that paralysed guy Justin told us you met when he was here with his ankle?'

To her surprise, Toni felt herself blushing as she nodded. 'I suppose they must be from him although I can't think how he knows I am here.' She thought for a moment, then said, 'Unless it was his doctor who told him. He saw me being brought along the corridor when I arrived and I'm pretty sure he recognized me because he nodded his head and smiled.'

'What does the card say?' Gemma asked.

Toni removed the card, which said, *For my very kind visitor. Get better soon. Aaron Osborn.*

'Clever guy getting the nurse to buy them for him, presumably on her way to work this morning,' Gemma said. She handed the note back to Toni. 'Must be pretty lonely lying in a bed all day with no one to talk to other than staff. I suppose he's hoping you'll be able to visit him again when you are up and about. I can't think of anything worse than being paralysed, can you? Do you want me to go and see him? Take a thank-you note or something?'

'That would be really kind,' Toni replied. 'You can say I'll try and see him before I'm discharged.'

When Toni had written her thank-you note and handed it to Gemma, Aaron Osborn had been temporarily forgotten. Instead

Gemma asked how Toni and Justin had met, and Toni found that talking about him and their whirlwind romance brought back the comfortable feeling of closeness to him. She told Gemma about the visit to her parents and their wish that she and Justin should wait to get married until they had known each other longer.

Gemma, to Toni's surprise, agreed with them. 'It isn't until you've lived with a man for some time that you find out what he is really like!' she commented. 'Besides which, Toni, things aren't the same as they were in our parents' day. These days you and Justin can live together as a couple without shocking anyone, so why rush into marriage unless you are one hundred per cent sure you are suited?'

She did not add that she and Peter had discussed the younger couple and questioned how long their affair would last. Justin was a strong, forceful young man: decisive, quick thinking and at times capable of being quick tempered. He was a very masculine man but in some ways a trifle immature. Toni, on the other hand, they judged to be quiet, thoughtful and sensitive. In some ways very much the daughter of older, old-fashioned parents. When Peter had summed up their differences, he had also reminded her that very often opposites did attract, and one complemented the other.

It was easy to understand why they were attracted to one another, he maintained. As for the unfortunate incident with the Spanish film star, it was not Justin's fault that the woman had made a beeline for him, and not surprising that Toni had been a bit put out. It didn't mean they weren't suited to be married.

Seeing that Toni was looking very tired, Gemma said she would take the thank-you note along to Aaron Osborn and return the following morning to see if Toni would be allowed to travel home. Peter, she promised, would telephone the hospital and, if a decision had been made, he would book her flight home for that afternoon and come with Gemma and her big suitcase to the hospital to drive her to the airport.

It was, however, a further twenty-four hours before Toni's doctor agreed to discharge her. In the meantime, Justin texted her three times, the last from Kennedy Airport to say he had arrived in the States. She was to go home to her parents' house to recuperate, he insisted, and not attempt to return to work too soon. The remainder of the text referred to the fun he was having with his friends and how much they were looking forward to the golf. It ended with his usual numerous endearments and kisses.

Try as she might, Toni could not prevent the slight feeling of resentment which followed after she had read these texts. She knew she was being unreasonable but at the same time she realized that, had it not been for Gemma's visit, she would have felt totally abandoned.

Her eyes were drawn to the beautiful display of white roses on the windowsill. She felt comforted by them. She would, she told herself, make a point of going to see Aaron Osborn before she left the hospital the following day. He probably wished he had someone to show they cared about him just as much as she wished Justin had sacrificed his own plans to take care of her.

NINE

The following day, with an hour to go before Gemma and Peter came to take her to the airport, Toni decided she had time to pay a quick visit to Aaron Osborn to say goodbye. She found him looking astonishingly cheerful, which she remarked upon as she sat down beside his bed. Having thanked him again for the beautiful roses, she asked him how he was feeling.

Unexpectedly he gave her a radiant smile and replied: 'My surgeon has just told me I can be flown home next week – well, not home but to Stoke Mandeville Hospital in Amersham, for rehabilitation, whatever that entails. He seems to think I might regain the full use of my arms and legs but warned me it was going to take time.' He reached out and touched her hand. 'See? I can move this arm a little already and, less pleasantly, I can feel the pain from some of my nasty bruises.'

He gave a long sigh. 'I can't begin to tell you how good it is to know I won't be facing a life where I can't do anything for myself.'

Toni returned his smile. 'I'm so happy for you! Do they say how long you might have to stay in Stoke Mandeville?'

The smile left Aaron's eyes. '*Señor* Cuevas said it was impossible to speculate. Depends on me to some extent, I suppose.'

'Do you have a job? One they will keep open for you?' Toni asked. The frown returned to Aaron's face.

'I thought of completing my law degree but I'm no longer sure whether I want to spend the rest of my life cooped up in an office sorting out other people's legal problems.'

He might very well have an unpleasant legal problem of his own when he was back in England, he told himself. He and Leena had signed their wills in favour of each other when they were married, but all his wife's assets were in India. How long would it be before that could be sorted?

His father-in-law had written to him from India saying that

during his brief stay in Spain he had instructed a Spanish lawyer in Malaga to look into the cause of the accident. His daughter, he wrote, was not a skiing novice and would not have undertaken a treacherous descent had she not first been assured it was safe to do so. Since the authorities in Pradollano had not put up adequate warning signs, it was his intention to take appropriate action to sue them. Meanwhile, he had also written to enquire why Leena's ashes had not yet been sent to him in India.

The official inquest established that the black run in question had been deemed fit for skiers, and that an appropriate warning was put out at the approach to the bend where Leena's and Aaron's falls had occurred. It was thereby established that Leena's death and Aaron's injuries were not the result of any negligence on behalf of the ski resort.

What Aaron did not tell Toni was that he had also received a letter from the family's Indian solicitor informing him that his father-in-law had withdrawn the standing order for the monthly allowance he'd given Leena when she married, and that her investments in India had been frozen because probate had not yet been granted.

It had always been clear to Aaron that Leena's father suspected him of marrying her for her money, and for that reason he had avoided any unnecessary contact with the man. Leena had laughed the matter off, saying that no husband would ever have been good enough for her doting father's only child.

He looked up now at the pretty girl sitting beside him and said, 'You can't know how much I have appreciated your visits. Selfishly, I can't help wishing you were not about to go home! You're my only visitor, you see. Will your boyfriend be there to meet you or will he still be in the States on his golfing holiday?'

Toni's face clouded as she replied that Justin would not be returning to England until the end of the following week.

'Brave man!' Aaron said caustically. 'If I were in his shoes I wouldn't risk letting such a pretty girl out of my sight a moment longer than I had to!'

Toni laughed. 'Believe me, I won't have any time to get up to mischief when I'm back in England. I'm a PA to the editor of a beauty magazine called *Temptation*. She wasn't very happy when I told her I couldn't go back to work for yet another week on top of my fortnight's summer holiday. She hates working with temps.'

As Aaron seemed interested, she continued, 'Her name is Julia and she's quite strict, but basically very kind as well as clever, and she's hugely successful at her job. I like working for her and there are lots of perks! She always gives me first choice of all the sample beauty products sent in to the magazine in the hope we will give them a favourable mention.'

His visitor had the most delightful smile, Aaron thought as he said gallantly: 'You most certainly prove their effectiveness. All the Spanish medics who attend to me ask when *la bella señorita* will visit me again. They think you are my girlfriend,' he added with a smile.

Toni was surprised to find herself blushing, and shrugged off the compliment.

There followed a moment of silence, then Aaron said, 'Are you going to marry your boyfriend? I see you aren't wearing an engagement ring.' Yet again, Toni found herself blushing and Aaron said quickly, 'You don't mind my asking, do you?'

'No, of course not! I do have a beautiful engagement ring, a diamond surrounded by little diamonds, but I haven't worn it outside the hotel in case I lose it. We haven't decided on a date yet.'

'He's a lucky guy!' Aaron said. 'I can tell you this much – if I were in his shoes, no way would I have left you to fend for yourself in hospital in a foreign country.'

Toni flushed, the remark striking just a little too close to her own secret thoughts – unfair thoughts which she had firmly put to the back of her mind as it had been Toni herself who had persuaded Justin to return home.

'Justin knows we have two very capable friends staying in our hotel who are looking after me,' she said defensively. 'They will be picking me up in about an hour to take me to the airport and see me safely on my way home. And for the record, Justin did offer to stay with me and I wouldn't let him.'

She made to stand up as she spoke but Aaron said quickly, 'Don't go, please! I didn't mean to offend you. It was very rude of me to comment on something which was none of my business. Forgive me, please?'

Toni hesitated, her feelings confused. She had been thoroughly thrown by Aaron's comment, yet at the same time she didn't want to leave him feeling embarrassed and upset when he was only saying what he thought. Wordless, she sat down.

'I've been hoping so much we could be friends,' Aaron said. 'I know you must have a hundred and one things to do in England, with your work and everything, but it would give me so much pleasure if we could communicate from time to time. I expect most of the patients at Stoke Mandeville get visitors, letters, that kind of thing, but the friends my wife and I had . . . well, they were really more her friends than mine, you know? The high society, "women-who-lunch" type. I can't think of a single one who would take time to visit me in hospital the way you have done out here.' He gave a deep, tremulous sigh. 'Now you'll be thinking I'm a hopeless wimp who should stop feeling sorry for himself. Just forget what I've been saying. A Christmas card will suffice! I'll text you my address once I know where I'll be.'

Without waiting for Toni to comment, he continued, 'As soon as I can, I plan to sell our penthouse as it could be months if not years before Stoke Mandeville perform miracles and get me sufficiently mobile to live on my own again.' He broke off, an apologetic smile on his good-looking face.

Filled once more with pity, Toni reminded herself that this was not only a seriously injured man, but a very lonely one. He had just lost his wife in a shocking accident, and clearly she had been the dominant force in their marriage. Their friends were hers rather than his, so he had no one to give him support when he most needed it.

She reached across the bed cover and took one of his hands in hers. 'Please forgive me if I am repeating myself when I say I am really so very sorry about the sad loss of your wife. One of the nurses told me of the dreadful accident and how you had been hoping to save her when you, too, fell down the mountainside. I admire you enormously for being so brave in such horrible circumstances.'

It was a minute or two before Aaron spoke. Then he said quietly, 'It was, of course, an appalling thing to happen and I shall always blame myself for not gauging the safety of the run where the accident happened. Every night I pray my poor Leena did not suffer before she died. She and I . . . well, we'd reached a point a couple of years into our marriage where we really didn't have anything much in common. We had finally decided we'd call it a day as a married couple but that we would always remain the very best of friends. It was on those terms we came on the skiing trip together, as it's the one activity we both enjoyed.' He gave a wry smile. 'At least Leena has been spared the tedium of having to look after a helpless cripple.'

He was silent for a minute before saying: 'Unfortunately, Leena didn't have much time for the friends I had in my bachelor days, and after we were married I gradually lost touch with them, so I expect it's going to be a bit lonely for a while until I'm fit again and able to make a new life for myself.'

His voice was not self-pitying but quietly matter-of-fact, and Toni said genuinely, 'I think you are being very brave about . . . everything. I'm sure things will get better . . . you will get better and you'll be able to make a new life for yourself with new friends. Meanwhile, I'd be happy to be considered one of them. I know Justin will want to meet you, and as you say we can keep in touch by text. And if possible, Justin and I will try to get to Stoke Mandeville to see how you are progressing. Justin loves any excuse to drive me around in his Alfa Romeo. If it's possible, we could take you out for lunch or something.'

'What a wonderful idea!' Aaron said, only just managing a smile. Obviously this charming, sympathetic, pretty girl had no idea that it was she he wanted to see, not her boyfriend. She was the kind of girl he should have married, he told himself. He was momentarily overcome by the bitter realization that there were impossible barriers in the way of any possibility of a future relationship with Toni. Quite apart from his physical disabilities, she already had a boyfriend – albeit one who seemed to take her very much for granted.

It was only after Toni had left that his feeling of despair gave way to a glimmer of hope. His doctor had said that there was every possibility he might regain full use of his limbs in the future. By then, Leena's will would have been executed, enabling him to be financially independent. Provided Toni had not married her boyfriend in the meantime, there would be nothing to prevent his pursuit of her. He had, he realized, for the first time in his life, fallen hopelessly in love.

Two hours later, sitting in the cramped seat of the aeroplane flying her back to England, Toni was engaged in friendly conversation with the elderly woman sitting next to her. The woman, a grandmother, had been particularly interested in hearing about Toni's holiday as she had a granddaughter the same age currently on holiday in Barcelona. It was only after they had landed and were waiting in a long queue for the suitcases to come off the luggage carousel at Gatwick Airport that Toni realized her conversation had been almost exclusively about the hospital patient, Aaron, and his shocking accident and bereavement. She had only mentioned Justin when her elderly companion had remarked upon her engagement ring. She looked down at her mobile to see if there was a new text from him.

A sharp stab of disappointment mixed with resentment shot through her as she saw there was no message. However awkward it might have been to text her on a golf course, it was surely not impossible, she told herself as the luggage carousel began to move. She had texted him the time her plane was landing at Gatwick so he could at least have sent a line or two saying welcome home or something similar. Perhaps she had been too premature expecting one so soon, she chided herself, but half an hour later, as she stood on the platform waiting for the train to London, she looked at her mobile again and the only message was from Aaron Osborn in Spain, saying that he trusted she had a good flight and thanking her once again for her kind visits.

Inexplicably, Toni felt another sudden wave of resentment. If this man, who was all but a complete stranger, could be bothered to text her, why couldn't Justin have found time to do so?

'I'm being stupid!' she chided herself once again. Aaron had nothing else to do – indeed, nothing else he *could* do – whereas Justin was probably surrounded by a crowd of guys demanding his attention and had simply forgotten the time. She would hear from him later.

All the same, she decided as the train pulled into the station, she would not – as would have been natural for her – text Justin to say she was safely back in England.

Even as the thought crossed her mind, a second thought followed. Would Justin even notice that she hadn't texted him? Or was he having far too much fun without her and hating the thought of having to come home?

TEN

Julia Nilson regarded her young assistant anxiously. Toni looked very pale and there were dark shadows under her eyes. She hoped she was not hatching flu or suffering a recurrence of the illness which had necessitated her brief stay in the Spanish hospital while on holiday. Not only was she hardworking and highly efficient, but Julia had grown personally fond of her. She had no children of her own and now, after working hours, treated Toni more as a goddaughter than an employee. Toni welcomed the relationship, the large age gap between herself and her mother making it difficult to confide her personal concerns to her.

Temptation magazine, of which Julia was the editor, was one of the bestselling journals on the market for young women. Julia had been offered the job of 'rescuing' it five years previously when its sales had diminished so seriously that it had been on the verge of being closed down. Julia was consequently very busy, but, despite the inconvenience to herself, she had authorized Toni's request for two weeks' holiday. Now, regarding Toni's pale face, the shadows beneath her eyes and the restless way she kept twisting her engagement ring round and round on her finger, it struck Julia that the beautiful set of wine glasses she had planned to give Toni and Justin for their wedding must remain hidden until some future date. All Toni had told her since her return from Spain was that a date had not yet been fixed, as her parents were insisting upon a longer engagement.

Pushing aside the fashion photos awaiting her approval, Julia looked anxiously at Toni's wistful face. 'Not probing, sweetie,' she said gently, 'but if there's something wrong – well, you know, a trouble shared is a trouble halved, and all that!'

Toni gave a half-hearted smile. Julia's sympathetic voice had brought her perilously close to tears.

'I feel such a wimp!' she said in a choked voice. 'Ever since I was quite little, I always believed I could cope with things – make them turn out the way I wanted. And by and large, they did! Like you choosing me to be your PA.' She smiled shakily. 'I knew I wasn't really qualified for it and I'll never stop being grateful to you for giving me the chance to prove I could do it. Now . . . well, being in love . . . it's sort of undermining, isn't it? I keep getting the feeling Justin doesn't really love me the way I love him.' She drew a deep sigh before adding: 'We just don't seem always to see things the same way. He's always saying he loves me, that he doesn't mean to hurt me, but . . .' Toni stopped talking as the tears started to fall.

Julia pushed a box of tissues across the desk. 'Hurt you? Not physically?' she said, shocked.

Toni smiled through her tears. 'No, of course not! It's just . . . well, I expect I'm being silly but at the weekend when he got back from America, all he could talk about was his golf and the fun he'd had with his mates and . . . well, he barely mentioned me and how I'd managed in that hospital in Spain on my own, and . . .' She broke off for a moment to blow her nose. 'He says if I won't agree to marry him until next year, I should at least let out my flat and move in with him, but . . .'

She broke off and Julia regarded her questioningly.

'But what? You haven't fallen out of love with him, have you? This isn't just a matter of pique because he so obviously enjoyed himself without you?'

Toni gave a half-hearted smile. 'I suppose that does come into it, but what hurt me was the way he dismissed our holiday as a bit of a failure – never once mentioned all the good times, or how I'd coped when he hurt his ankle and then him leaving me alone in that hospital. Julia, I know I'm being an idiot but, for whatever reason, I don't want to move in with him. I do love him . . . want to be with him. It's just that I've begun to think my parents were quite right – I haven't known Justin long enough to be absolutely certain about marrying him. Part of me is still desperately anxious to do so and then suddenly . . . well, I get this anxious feeling. Do you think I'm being a complete idiot?'

Julia's face was thoughtful as she watched Toni screw up her damp tissue and toss it into the wastepaper basket.

'No, I don't!' she said firmly. 'This isn't something I ever talk about but I rushed into marriage when I was twenty. He was incredibly attractive and I fell instantly – and irrationally, as it turned out – in love with him. It wasn't until after we were married that I discovered he was one of those men who have to be dominant and resort to violence when they can't get their own way. He was always sorry afterwards and begged me to forgive him and I did . . . until I got pregnant. Because of what he did to me, I lost my baby. So I divorced him.'

Julia looked intensely sad for a moment, then added thoughtfully: 'Maybe you should move in with Justin . . . find out what it would be like being married to him. In my experience, lovers are a very different kettle of fish from husbands!'

Despite her depression, Toni drew out another tissue, blew her nose and smiled. 'My mum likes to think she's really with it, but she would be quite shocked if she heard the advice you're giving me! Believe it or not, she and Dad thought Justin and I had separate bedrooms when we were on holiday!'

Julia returned her smile before asking: 'I assume no problems with your sex life?'

Toni shook her head. 'Absolutely not! The sex – well, it's really the main thing in our relationship. Even when I'm cross with Justin about something, he only has to look at me in that certain way he has and we're back in bed making love. I sometimes wonder what it would be like if we weren't so attracted to one another.'

For a fleeting second, Toni had a flash of memory of Justin dancing with the voluptuous Spanish actress in the hotel nightclub. Later that night, in bed, he'd admitted he'd found the woman attractive and might have been tempted to have a fling with her if he'd not been in love with Toni. She herself could not imagine being attracted sexually to any other man – not even the attractive invalid in the hospital in Spain. Though she did admit to herself that there had been something mesmerizing about his unusual grey eyes – the way they had seemed to look deep into her innermost emotions, understanding them despite them being virtual strangers.

Somewhat to Toni's surprise, Aaron Osborn had texted her on three subsequent occasions: the first after she had visited him before leaving the hospital to get her flight home; the second when a date had been fixed for him to be flown home to Stoke Mandeville Hospital at the end of the month. The last one, which she had received that morning, sent from the hospital in England, expressed his hope that she might be able to find time to visit him one day when she had nothing better to do. The place might interest her, he'd added, and a visit would relieve the boredom of the daily routine imposed on him.

When Toni had suggested to Justin that they might drive down to Amersham one weekend and pay a brief call on Aaron, he had been far from keen on the idea, pointing out that not only were there Newmarket and Ascot races he wanted to take her to, but he had two golf competitions pending which would involve three weekends. If she felt it was so important to see the unfortunate patient, she should go on her own or take one of her girlfriends with her.

'I suppose his suggestion isn't unreasonable,' she said now to Julia as she relayed the current state of her relationship with Justin. 'Maybe I will go down to Stoke Mandeville and visit that poor guy. He told me he had not kept in touch with his school friends and his more recent friends were mostly his wife's. Apparently he did get masses of letters of condolence from them when they learned of the dreadful accident which killed her, but I gather not one has bothered to visit him in Stoke Mandeville.'

'What about work colleagues?' Julia asked curiously.

Toni shook her head. 'He's not employed; he was finishing his law training at a college in London but left when he got married, partly because his wife wanted to travel. They were married six months after they met.'

'That was a bit quick!' Julia commented. 'They must have been very much in love.'

Toni nodded. 'He didn't talk about her very much. I suppose he was still in shock when I visited him in that Spanish hospital. I felt so sorry for him. At least he isn't totally paralysed as he'd thought was the case the first time I saw him.'

Julia was regarding her thoughtfully. 'Sounds like your pity for this guy is affecting your emotional equilibrium!' she said. 'He may be extremely brave and all that, but by the sound of it your Justin is a bit jealous! I expect he wants you to watch him win his golf trophy or whatever, and considers it preferable to driving fifty-odd miles to visit a virtual stranger – and a man at that!'

Toni looked surprised. 'He's hardly jealous of a bedridden invalid, surely,' she commented dryly.

'Maybe an "invalid", but one you told me was recovering. And Toni, you went to great lengths to tell me what fascinating grey eyes he has and the trouble he had gone through to send you those roses, and so on. Come to that, why should you, a total stranger, have taken it upon yourself to befriend him?'

Toni frowned. 'What harm is there in that?' she asked. 'Justin was enjoying himself in America with his golf chums so he didn't need my attention.'

Julia regarded the younger girl thoughtfully. 'Are you saying you don't think Justin needs you?'

Toni's frown deepened. 'Yes, in bed!' she said. 'I've come to the conclusion that for him sex is the most important part of our relationship.'

Julia shrugged her shoulders, a slight smile lighting up her face. 'So what is unusual about that, dear girl! Find me any young man of Justin's age for whom sex is not their priority when they're with the girl they love. He wants to marry you, Toni, for heaven's sake!'

Toni scowled. 'I don't think he cares about getting married any more. All he wants is for me to move into his flat so we can make love whenever we feel like it, or he feels like it! But I'm not moving in with him. My mother was absolutely right when she said we hadn't known each other long enough to take that final step – at least, what one hopes will be final. If Justin really does love me the way I need him to, then it won't hurt him to wait another year, will it?'

Julia's gaze was now sceptical. Was it Justin's faithfulness which was in question, or Toni's? Was Toni somehow confusing sympathy for Aaron Osborn with a more romantic emotion? As far as she, Julia, was aware, Justin was a typical young English guy who found it easier to express his deepest emotions in bed. Toni was young for her age and Justin was her first serious boyfriend. Her parents were probably quite right to persuade her to delay a year before taking the final step, but her decision not to move in with him in the meantime did seem questionable. After all, there was no better way to find out if a couple was sufficiently compatible to spend the rest of their lives together.

Toni now handed back the box of tissues as she attempted a smile at her boss. 'I feel awful taking up so much of your time offloading my concerns,' she said apologetically. 'All I can say for certain, Julia, is that I won't suddenly give up my job, and that's a promise. I love working here with you and I can't imagine ever having a better, kinder boss.'

Touched by the obvious sincerity in the younger girl's voice, Julia replied: 'I appreciate your loyalty, Toni, and I want you to know that if you have any more personal problems, I'm always here to listen.' She smiled. 'I may not have much experience as an agony aunt, but sometimes it can be helpful simply to spell out one's worries to someone else. Just remember, Toni, there's no hurry. As the old saying goes, "If in doubt, don't". More often than not, one's instinct is right.'

As if prearranged, the telephone on Julia's desk started ringing. Realizing it was a personal call, Toni gathered up the folders she was carrying and quietly left the room. Sitting down at her desk in the adjoining room, she pulled her in-tray towards her. With an effort, she stifled her feelings of gratitude to the kind employer who had befriended her when she was most in need of advice, and settled down belatedly to work.

ELEVEN

L ying in Justin's arms in the spacious bedroom in his flat
in Egerton Gardens, Toni told herself that she was being
totally unreasonable refusing to move in with him. A
colleague at work had asked her if she knew of a furnished flat
available to rent in Fulham, where Toni currently lived, and the
girl would make an ideal tenant if Toni leased it to her. Justin
would probably refuse to take any rent money towards her keep
in his spacious accommodation, and fear of this loss of her
independence was one of the reasons prompting her reluctance
to move in with him.

As if divining her thoughts, Justin yet again brought up the
subject. One arm encircling her waist, his lips nuzzling her
bare shoulder, he said, 'You aren't going to need your flat in
any case, my beloved one.' He smiled. 'I haven't told you yet
but I've got some ace news.'

Toni had arrived after work and, as usual, Justin had whisked
her straight off to bed. And, as usual, although Toni thought his
impatience flattering in one way, she wished they could have had
a drink and a chat first. Now that their love-making was over,
he was eager to impart his news.

'Dad's bought a yacht – a hundred and seventy footer!' he
told her, his eyes shining with excitement. 'He's planning to sail
round the world . . . Barbados, Mexico, Honolulu, Tahiti,
Australia, Japan, China . . . you name it. He plans to stop off
wherever he and Ma fancy, and to be away for about a year.'

'Sounds fantastic!' Toni said, reminding herself that Justin's
parents were extremely rich people who could well afford such
luxuries.

'The thing is,' Justin was saying excitedly, 'they want us to go
with them. Dad said he'll find someone else to replace me in the
office. Just think, babe, it will be like an awesome honeymoon.'

Unaware that Toni's body had stiffened, he continued: 'They
want to get away in a few weeks – beginning of July, so you'll

have to give in your notice at that magazine of yours pretty quickly. Wow, hon! Just think – China, Egypt – places I've always wanted to visit.' He chuckled. 'I expect Ma put Dad up to it. She's a travelholic. If that's the right word. Good old Dad, always ready for a new adventure . . .'

He broke off, now finally aware that Toni's body had stiffened. Was she too excited to say anything? When she did speak, her words came as such a shock, he supposed that he must have misheard her.

'Say again,' he said uneasily.

It was a moment or two before Toni could gather enough courage to repeat what she had said. Her voice trembling, she whispered, 'I can't go with you, Justin. I just can't! Julia, my boss . . . she's been incredibly good to me. She didn't once complain about that extra week I was convalescing after I got back from Spain. I can't simply walk out and leave her before she can find a replacement for me.'

Justin sat up abruptly and, swinging his legs over the side of the bed, reached for his jeans before turning back to face her. His voice was dangerously quiet as he said, 'You can't be serious! How can you turn down the chance of a lifetime to go round the world? Because that's what this is! You just can't! We'd be together . . .' His voice shook as he pulled his T-shirt over his head and stared down at her.

'Surely that woman you work for would understand?' he demanded. 'You're always telling me what a decent person she is. We won't be leaving for at least a week or two, so surely she can find a replacement by then?' He paused and looked intently at Toni, then said quietly, 'Don't you *want* to come with me?'

Toni felt the sting of tears behind her eyes as she replied: 'Of course I want to . . . of course I do, but I can't leave Julia in the lurch. Can't I fly out and join you later? When she's found a replacement and had time to show her the ropes?'

Justin turned away, his face suddenly taut with disappointment. 'The way you're talking, Toni, it seems this wretched woman is more important to you than I am. Well, Mum and Dad are really looking forward to spending time with me, and I haven't the slightest intention of disappointing them since I'm clearly second in line of importance to you.'

Toni's mouth tightened and her eyes narrowed as she got up from the bed and started to put on her clothes. Her voice was all but inaudible as she said, 'It isn't a matter of who comes first, but what comes first. Please try to understand, Justin. It took Julia at least six weeks to train me into the job. She was incredibly patient and understanding, and she treats me more like a daughter than an employee. I could join you just as soon as I was sure she had a suitable replacement for me. Maybe I could even persuade her to take someone else on for a year so I could return when we got back to England.' Her voice trailed into silence as she saw the expression on Justin's face.

'I thought we were supposed to be getting married next year!' His voice was now anything but loving. 'Or is that on the back burner, too? I'm beginning to wonder whether you really do love me.' His voice hardened. 'Dammit, Toni, if your parents hadn't dissuaded you we'd have been married before we went to Spain . . . our honeymoon, supposedly, or had you forgotten?'

Toni quickly brushed away her tears with the back of her hand. 'Maybe the boot is on the other foot and *you* don't love *me!*' she said. 'I do realize that my reaction to your news must be horribly disappointing, Justin, but I thought you would understand. Of course I want to go – it's a fantastic invitation – but I couldn't enjoy myself knowing I'd left Julia in the lurch. Surely you would feel the same were you in my shoes?' Her voice softened. 'I'll fly out and join you as soon as I possibly can, I promise. Maybe Julia will find someone before you go. Please don't be cross, Justin. You must know how much I want to be with you, and a cruise round the world – well, I can't think of anything more magical.'

Justin grimaced and looked at her with narrowed eyes. 'Seems that my feelings come a very poor second to your boss's,' he said childishly. 'Frankly, Toni, I'm beginning to doubt whether you do really love me. You won't even move in here with me when it's quite obviously the sensible thing for you to do – what any girl would do if she was in love. We're engaged to be married, for God's sake!'

For a moment, Toni was silenced. Even Julia had been surprised by her reluctance to move in with her boyfriend. Come to that, she could not understand it herself – her vague wish to retain her independence for a while longer. As for the opportunity to sail round the world with Justin – well, no doubt a lot of people would think her ripe for a psychiatric ward for not giving in her notice to Julia rather than delaying the start of a world cruise with the man she was soon going to marry.

Toni's expression changed as she walked across the room and put her arms round Justin's waist. She leaned her face against his chest.

'Please try to understand!' she said. 'Of course I want to come with you, be with you, and I can't think of any more wonderful way of spending a year than travelling round the world with you in a private yacht. It's hugely generous of your parents to invite me, and of course I'll come. I'll join you just as soon as I possibly can . . . a month maybe . . . or a few weeks . . . that's all . . . It will give me time, too, to warn my parents that I'll be away.'

The memory of her mother's last phone call suddenly came back to her. She had mentioned some tests her father was having done, 'just to be on the safe side', she'd said. But when Toni had asked for more details, her mother had replied evasively: 'Nothing to worry about, darling. He sends his love.'

She would go down to Cherry Tree Cottage to see them next weekend, she decided. Maybe Justin would go with her if he didn't have a golf date. He and one of his friends had been playing in a knock-out competition and were doing remarkably well. It now looked as if they might end up in the final play-off, so they were practising as often as they could.

Justin's voice softened as he swept back a strand of light-brown hair from Toni's forehead. 'How long do you really think it will be before you can join us?' he asked.

Toni regarded him uneasily. 'Oh, darling, I honestly don't know. There'll be lots of applicants for my job but it has to be someone Julia takes to. I can't really guess . . . it depends,' she ended vaguely. In a brighter tone, she added: 'You said you wouldn't be leaving for several weeks, so it's always possible Julia could have found someone suitable by then, and I'll be able to go with you.'

She didn't really believe in the possibility, because she knew that Julia would want to have a new PA on at least a month's approval. But Justin was looking a great deal happier.

'That sounds more like it!' he said. 'Silly of me, I suppose, but you had me worried just now that you didn't want to go. I did wonder if you didn't fancy being with my parents . . .'

'Oh, no, of course not!' Toni interrupted. 'You know I like them both very much, and it's wonderfully kind of them to include me on the trip. You will get them to understand – about Julia, I mean, won't you? You understand now, Justin, don't you?'

'I suppose! My mother will think you are crazy, but Dad will approve. He thinks most young people these days are entirely selfish.' He paused momentarily, then said quietly, 'You do still love me, don't you, babe?'

Toni flung her arms round his neck and kissed him. 'Of course I do! Of course! And as for going round the world with you on a yacht – well, it's like a dream. I'll tell Julia first thing on Monday morning and maybe . . . just maybe . . . she will find someone before you leave.'

Justin's handsome face lit up in a huge smile as he said fervently, 'Keeping my fingers crossed. Here, look at this!'

He crossed the room to the table which served as his desk and held out a piece of paper which had been printed from his computer. 'It's a list of all the places my parents are planning to go. You must get some new clothes, Toni – bikinis, hot weather stuff. And you don't have to worry about being able to afford it: Dad's put a thousand pounds into my account to spend on the trip for shopping, souvenirs, snorkels and so on.' Seeing the expression on Toni's face, he said sternly, 'And he says you are not to spend one penny of your own money. He says as we're getting married, you are almost part of the family and he's treating you like a daughter-in-law.'

'But, Justin . . .' Toni got no further as Justin hurried back to her and covered her face with kisses. The cruise, Julia . . . all were forgotten as Justin pulled her over to the bed and down beside him.

'I shall absolutely hate being without you those first weeks,' he whispered. 'Promise me you'll come the very first moment you can.'

It was as she made that promise that the thought struck Toni: if he really would be unhappy without her, why did he not stay with her instead of leaving her behind?

TWELVE

Aaron lent back in his chair, his eyes closed as the sun's rays warmed his face. He was outside the hospital in the garden breathing fresh air untainted by the smell of antiseptic that pervaded his ward and the corridors. It was now four months since the fall which he'd thought had paralysed him for the rest of his life, yet here he was, able to use all his limbs, albeit with the aid of intensive physiotherapy and a walking frame. The transformation from those frightening, black days of despair was astonishing. Everything in his life seemed to have turned the corner and be evolving in his favour.

First, there was his recovery – something which, he'd been assured, would progress to full mobility provided he was patient and did as his doctors told him. Next came the letter he had been eagerly awaiting from his solicitors. He'd been aware that his father-in-law mistrusted his motives for marrying Leena. Somehow he had managed to do a credit check on him and discovered that he was virtually penniless and without an established career. Consequently he'd assumed, correctly, that he had married Leena for her money. After the accident, when the terms of her will were disclosed, he'd written to Aaron saying he intended to challenge its validity.

Last week, to Aaron's intense relief, his solicitor's letter had arrived, advising him that his father-in-law had no legal justification for challenging Aaron's right to inherit all of Leena's assets. Now he felt assured that if he handled her investments cleverly, he need never have to work to support himself. Even her beautiful penthouse flat in Mayfair now belonged to him – not that he intended to live in it. He had no desire to be reunited with her friends. Amongst them, there had been several wealthy society wives who, despite their intimacy with Leena, had invited him to enjoy 'an otherwise boring afternoon', as they termed it, in bed with them.

He'd known ever since he'd reached adulthood that he was

attractive to women. He had more than his fair share of sex appeal, Leena had once said as she'd described his attributes. He'd been accustomed all his life to the advantage he had over most other men, and had taken it as normal when the nurses in the hospital in Malaga and at Stoke Mandeville gave him that little bit extra care and attention.

Now he was looking at his mobile phone, at a message he had read at least six times. It was from Antonia Ward – Toni, the girl who had visited him in those agonizing first weeks in the Malaga hospital when he'd thought he'd be paralysed for the rest of his life. He had not expected to hear from her again after she had returned to England, but she had said she might visit him if ever she was in the region of Stoke Mandeville. Now, miraculously, she had contacted him to say she was going to a school friend's evening wedding in Aylesbury and, as she would be staying overnight, could call in to see him the following morning if it was convenient.

He had never forgotten her. Although she was not conventionally beautiful, there was something about her which he found hard to define – large brown eyes which lit up when she smiled but were otherwise deep, mysterious pools which made him wonder what she was thinking and feeling. When she'd left his hospital room, it had felt as if the light had suddenly gone out and left him in a dark chasm of despair.

Could he possibly have fallen in love with this girl, Toni, who was almost a stranger? He was aware she had a boyfriend – a guy who'd gone off on a golfing holiday leaving her alone in a foreign hospital. No competition there! Was it possible that, in the brief few hours they were to spend having lunch together, he could make her see him not as a hospital patient but as a man? She had spoken of visiting him with her boyfriend, but by the sound of it he was not going to be with her today.

His glanced down at the shirt he was wearing – fashionable, with large blue and white checks which Leena had bought for him from the Tommy Hilfiger shop. She had scorned most of his existing wardrobe which, because of his limited bank balance, was mostly from high street outlets. The soft grey cotton of his chinos complemented the colour of his eyes, she had maintained, adding that she wanted all her female friends to be frantically jealous of her having a husband who was better looking than David Beckham, and who dressed as well.

Aaron had never cared much about his choice of clothes. There had been no need: women had made themselves available regardless. Today, however, he'd found himself considering his appearance quite seriously. He'd shaved particularly carefully and had his hair cut – not too short – the day before. Fortunately, it was an unexpectedly fine summer and, by spending as much time as he was allowed out of doors, his hospital pallor had turned to a light tan.

Would Toni find him attractive now that he was so well on the road to recovery? The question seemed to be dominating his mind. Unable to endure the uncertainty of her time of arrival, he called up her number on his mobile. She texted almost immediately: *Hi, Aaron. I call 4 u 12ish. See u soon. Toni.*

'I call for you,' she'd said, not 'we' – so the boyfriend wouldn't be with her. Aaron's heart missed a beat. Would a few hours be long enough for him to gain her interest? She must have some feelings for him already, having kept in touch since those brief visits in Spain. He was well aware that at first she had regarded him merely with pity, but even after he'd told her he now hoped for a complete recovery, she had still kept in touch.

Glancing at his wristwatch, Aaron saw that it was nearly midday. For the first time in his life, his heart was beating furiously in eager anticipation of a woman's arrival. He was both excited and nervous lest the meeting did not go as he was hoping. Not only must he make himself attractive to her but he must find a way to belittle the boyfriend – find out more about him and persuade Antonia he wasn't the right man for her.

For a moment, Aaron's exhilaration deserted him as he faced the very real obstacles in his way, not the least of which was his health. He needed to be completely fit again, back in London leading an independent life; to set himself up in a decent flat where he could invite Toni for drinks before taking her out to dinner, to a musical, a nightclub. He'd buy a decent car – a Jaguar, maybe, so he could take her out for a day – whatever she wanted to see or do. He had one very big advantage: money. He could buy her expensive gifts . . . jewellery, clothes, perfumes – the kind of extravagances Leena used to choose with no regard for the cost.

While Aaron sat in the summer sunshine waiting for her, Toni was in her beloved old Golf, driving through the pretty village of Haddenham on her way to Stoke Mandeville. She, too, was lost in thought. This morning there had been another text from Justin. Their yacht, *Silver Sprite*, had just left Port Elizabeth and was now continuing its way up the east coast of South Africa towards Mozambique. His parents were in excellent spirits as they'd had a riotous last evening with South African friends who lived there.

Justin's text said that he was missing Toni dreadfully. When, he'd demanded, was she flying out to join them? It was now eight weeks since they'd left England and, unless he had missed one of her text messages, he gathered there had been no satisfactory replacement found for her as yet.

The wedding Toni had attended the previous day had had a strange effect upon her. In one way, she'd felt she would give everything to be the bride walking up the aisle to become Justin's wife. As far as she could ascertain from the itinerary he'd given her, he was now crossing the Indian Ocean, and it was almost impossible to believe that only five months ago they would have been married had it not been for her parents' concerns.

As Toni turned into the road leading to the hospital, she tried to put out of her mind the realization that it could be weeks before she could fly out to join Justin and his parents. Julia was doing her utmost not to be too picky but the candidates she had interviewed so far were very far from suitable, ranging from former undergraduates with English degrees to young girls who had left school at sixteen with no more than a few GCSEs to their names. Only one had the imaginative managerial skills and capacity to anticipate Julia's requirements – she seemed suitable and Julia had taken her on. Toni had just been making plans to join Justin when the girl suddenly decided she didn't like being what she called a 'gofer' and left.

As the days passed, Toni's longing to be with Justin intensified, and yesterday, watching the newly-weds as they danced lovingly in each other's arms at the reception, she'd found herself reflecting that Justin should not have gone away without her.

His loving texts sent without fail from every new destination were hugely welcome but no compensation for the sound of his voice, the feel of his arms round her, his kisses and embraces. She missed his love-making, too, and the memory of that last night before he left was still fresh in her memory. It had been completely spontaneous, the need to be physically united so overwhelming that they had reached a height of sexual passion beyond anything they had experienced before.

Afterwards, Justin had declared that she *must* leave with him – that if she did not, he would forgo the trip and stay with her as he could not bear to be apart from her. She had reminded him then with a smile that he'd managed to spend two very happy weeks golfing in America without her, but added more seriously that he would be upsetting his parents, who had planned the year's adventure as much for Justin's enjoyment as for their own.

When Stoke Mandeville Hospital came into sight, the thought crossed Toni's mind that her words had been vaguely prophetic. Among the dozen or so photos Justin had sent, in two of them he had been on a sandy palm-fringed beach enjoying what was obviously a nocturnal party. The group of young people were laughing, their arms around each other as they stood in a semi-circle against a backdrop of moonlit sea. Justin had his arms around two scantily clad girls in bikinis which barely covered their slim, tanned bodies. She knew it was silly to feel jealous, that Justin was part of a group having a good time, so what else would he appear to be but happy? There was no reason whatever why he shouldn't enjoy the company of girls, and if she had any sense she would enjoy the forthcoming lunch with Aaron Osborn, the good-looking patient who, by all accounts, was longing to see her.

Aaron, she now realized, must have been watching for her car, as he came out through the front door to greet her. For the briefest second, she did not recognize the tall, upright figure she had last seen as a helpless invalid in a hospital bed in Spain. He was so much taller than she had imagined, she thought, as she watched him walking towards her. He was wearing fashionably cut chinos, a blue-and-white checked shirt and carried a denim jacket over one arm. He had reached her side before she had locked the door.

'I recognized your car coming down the drive,' he said as he held out his hand. 'You said it was a green Golf so I knew it was you. Do you want to see round the hospital, or shall we go straight to the pub?'

Suddenly feeling ridiculously shy, Toni opted for the pub and drew back the hand he was still holding. This tall, self-assured, handsome individual bore little resemblance to the pale, rigid invalid who had looked so despairing, so helpless in the sterile hospital bed. How old was he? she wondered irrelevantly as she unlocked the car door and he helped her into the driving seat carefully as if she, not he, was the invalid. As he squeezed his long legs into the well of the passenger seat beside her, Toni said, 'It's really good to see you looking so fit! Stupidly, I wondered whether you might be in a wheelchair and if I could manage to get it into the back of the car.'

Aaron laughed. 'I would have warned you, Toni. It's OK for me to call you that, isn't it? I know your real name is Antonia, which, if the truth be told, I think is the prettier name of the two. It suits you, too.'

Toni felt herself blushing. 'Your name is unusual, isn't it?' She changed the subject. 'My book of names says there was a Celtic saint called Aaron and mentioned an English Aaron in 1199, but it didn't give a meaning. Of course, my name is the feminine form of Anthony, but obviously you knew that . . . I mean, if you'd thought about it, and why should you?'

She broke off, aware that she was blabbering. Discomfited by the realization, she almost took a left instead of a right turn at the approaching T-junction.

'I'm flattered that you bothered to research my name!' Aaron said smoothly, and to her relief, turned the conversation to the Woolpack pub which one of the doctors had recommended to him.

'I've been told the food here is really good,' he said as Toni drew to a halt in the car park. Without waiting for her reply, he got out of the car and hurried round to open the driver's door for her.

Toni eased her way out of her seat, conscious of Aaron's hand clasping hers. Inexplicably, the contact seemed oddly intimate and it suddenly occurred to her that Aaron's insistence on taking her out to lunch was not, perhaps, solely his way of thanking her, a stranger, for visiting him in hospital in Spain. She must make sure he understood that Justin was the love of her life and that he should not think of her as a potential girlfriend.

Guiding Toni towards the door of the restaurant, his arm beneath her elbow, Aaron's thoughts were similarly focused. This Justin, who she was expecting to marry, had conveniently departed on a world cruise. He had only to find some way to prevent Toni from joining the guy as she'd planned for him to have all the time he needed to take Justin's place.

If this thought had been in the back of his mind for weeks, seeing Toni today here, beside him, it now became an obsession. In ten days' time, he'd been told, he could be discharged from the hospital and could move into the large flat the estate agents had found for him in Clapham. From the pictures the agent had sent him, it was perfect: newly furnished and well equipped, looking over the common. Leena's penthouse flat had been sold as soon as probate was granted, so now he would have no commitments – nothing to take his time – and he would be free to do whatever was necessary to turn Toni's affections from her current boyfriend to him.

THIRTEEN

Toni had had no word from Justin for three days. She had tried to think of a reason for his silence – he'd forgotten to charge his mobile; there was no signal; he'd lost his phone. But, she told herself, he could have used his father's or mother's mobiles. However, this was the least pressing of her concerns, for she had just found out her father was desperately ill. He had been rushed into the local hospital having had a stroke.

As usual, Julia had been incredibly understanding when Toni had asked for time off to go home to support her shocked mother. For three days the doctors had been uncertain whether her father would survive, but he'd finally turned the corner, albeit with partial loss of speech and movement. Together with a helpful neighbour, Toni moved the spare bed downstairs into what had been the dining room, and the Red Cross promised to deliver a wheelchair and other aids he would require while convalescing.

Julia had suggested that Toni take Fridays and Mondays off work so that she would have half the week to help her mother. She herself could manage temporarily with Cynthia, one of the secretaries who had wanted to apply for the job when Toni first knew she would be leaving.

'It will be a useful chance to see if Cynthia can cope,' Julia had said. 'Now off you go and help that poor mother of yours. I remember you telling me once how totally devoted your parents are. Give her my best!'

Hoping she would not run out of petrol, Toni drove down the familiar road home, trying to rid herself of her depression. From the way things looked at the moment, it was doubtful if Cynthia would prove a suitable replacement for her. Yet again, Julia had been wonderful – an understanding, helpful friend as well as her boss – and Toni was as determined as ever not to leave her in the lurch.

Justin's last text had said that they had left the heat of the Red Sea and were now on their way up the Suez Canal to the

Mediterranean. They had taken an amusing French family on board at Suez who had been intending to fly home to France. Hopefully they would help to pass the time until Toni could join them. *If that time ever came*, he'd ended bitterly.

No wonder she felt so low, Toni thought as she watched for the turning off the motorway on to the Banbury road. She had been very lucky to have found such a good friend as Aaron Osborn. When she'd telephoned him to reject a dinner date on account of her father's stroke and the need for her to go home, he had immediately offered to drive her down to Hook Norton in his car, saying it would not be a good idea for her to be driving on the motorway when she was obviously shocked and worried.

At that time, Aaron had been out of hospital and living in London for several weeks. When he'd invited her out to dinner, he'd said he was very much at a loose end, and now a drive to the country would give him something to do.

Toni had declined his offer, not just because she felt quite capable of driving herself, but because she would need her car once she arrived home. Her mother's eyesight was deteriorating and, for some time now, only her father was licensed to drive their car.

Concentrating on the turning off the M40, Toni was on the familiar road leading to Banbury when her thoughts returned to the tasks awaiting her. For one thing, she would have to arrange something like the Hospital Volunteer Driving Bureau so that once she had joined Justin her mother could continue her visits to the hospital. The cost of the taxis she had been using was exorbitant.

Held up for a few minutes in a queue of cars, Toni's gaze was caught by a beautiful display of flowers outside a florist, and she was reminded of the Interflora bouquet Aaron had sent her mother when she'd told him how distressed she was. He really was an extremely kind and thoughtful man, she reflected. He'd also arranged for a large Harrods hamper of food to be delivered to the cottage, 'to lessen the bother of cooking', his note had said.

It was now obvious to Toni as she took a right turn to Bloxham that Aaron was not only an extremely wealthy man but a very generous one. On the two occasions he had taken her out to lunch since he'd been discharged from hospital, it had been to one of

London's most expensive restaurants. She thought suddenly of the last occasion when they were approached by a smartly dressed woman wearing a fabulous necklace and bracelet, and the highest heels Toni had ever seen outside advertisements. The woman had sauntered up to their table and, after a brief glance at Toni, said to Aaron: 'We've all been wondering what happened to you, Aaron. Douglas said he'd heard you were still stuck in that amputees' hospital, so I could hardly believe my eyes when I saw you sitting here with . . . with . . .?'

She had paused, staring at Toni, until Aaron had said in a stiff voice: 'This is Antonia Ward. Toni, may I introduce Fiona Astonbury-Jones.'

The woman had held out a much-beringed hand and said coldly: 'Aaron's late wife, Leena, and I were best friends, you know. I, and all her friends, were completely *bouleversée* when we heard of that dreadful accident. We wondered . . . well, how you were coping, Aaron, but I see you've managed to come to terms with your ghastly loss.'

The remark had been so uncalled for, so bitingly said, it had sounded more like an accusation. Toni had not been surprised when Aaron had said sharply: 'I see your husband is looking this way, Fiona. Perhaps you should rejoin him.'

Clearly accepting this dismissal, Fiona had nevertheless remained standing, staring at Aaron as he'd resumed his seat. Then she'd said suddenly: 'Leena was such an experienced skier, we couldn't understand what made her choose that black run, or perhaps you chose it, Aaron?' And she'd turned on her heel and made her way back to the man patiently waiting for her.

Toni recalled Aaron's white face, his half-closed eyes and the trembling of his hands as he'd sought to control his anger at the remark which was not only insulting but extremely hurtful. She recalled how embarrassed she had been, how angry Aaron was, so much so that she'd seen his hands still trembling as he lifted his glass of wine to his lips. It had been several minutes before he regained his composure and told her that Fiona Astonbury-Jones was one of his wife's wealthy society friends who had expected Leena to marry at least a title, and had told Leena that their marriage would not last as they had nothing in common.

Although this had proved to be the case, it had not lessened

the terrible shock of the accident which had killed Leena, Aaron
had told her. Her death in so tragic an accident was something
he would never be able to forget.

Toni had no difficulty believing that he still grieved terribly
for his wife but, understandably, as her death had been so horri-
fying, he tried not to think about it. It was why he enjoyed Toni's
company, he said, because she was the very opposite in every
way to his late wife, as well as being so very different from
Leena's female friends.

Recalling his remark, it crossed Toni's mind that Aaron had
been perfectly right in thinking she was a very different type
from his wife's friend, the shrill-voiced, unpleasant female
who had spoken so hatefully to him. People did differ in
hundreds of ways, she reflected. Aaron and Justin were a perfect
example of opposites. Although she loved Justin dearly, enough
to want to be married to him and eventually have his children,
she was not blind to his faults. The impulsive streak in his
nature often made him thoughtless. At times it seemed as if
he had not entirely grown up yet, and that their life together
should follow the paths he chose rather than the way Toni
would prefer. As if by deliberate contrast, in the short time
she'd known Aaron, he had wanted only to please her, rather
than himself.

So deep in thought had Toni been that, having driven automatically through Bloxham, she nearly missed the right turn to Hook
Norton. Driving down the narrow twisting road to the pretty
Cotswold village, her thoughts turned to her father and how well
or otherwise he would recover from his stroke. Her mother had
sounded distraught on the telephone, but with their silver wedding
anniversary only a week away, it was inevitable that she would
panic if she feared she might lose her adoring and adored husband.

When Toni parked outside Cherry Tree Cottage, her mother
came hurrying out to greet her.

'Thank goodness you are here, my darling!' she said, hugging
Toni when her daughter had climbed out of the car. 'I was afraid
you might be detained at that office of yours. I've got lunch ready
so we can eat early and be sure to get to the hospital by two
thirty – that's the start of visiting time. I do so hope Daddy will
recognize you. He knows me, of course, but . . . Well, the doctor

says he is starting to get a little better . . .' She broke off, tears filling her eyes.

Toni decided it would be better to sound optimistic than to sympathize with her distraught mother. Following her into the cottage, she said brightly, 'I've bought one of those tiny miniature bottles of whisky for Dad. You know how he loves his "tot" as he calls it.'

Diverted by Toni's remark, the tears on Mrs Ward's cheeks ceased flowing. 'But, darling, you know they won't allow alcohol in hospital,' she said.

Toni smiled. 'I'll smuggle it in to him; pretend to put it in his bedside table where the doctors can't see it.'

A faint smile replaced the concern on Mrs Ward's face. 'Of course, you are quite right, darling. Just seeing it will cheer him up. What a clever thought!'

'Actually it wasn't my idea, it was Aaron's,' Toni admitted as she sat down opposite her mother at the kitchen table. 'Aaron Osborn, the man who was paralysed, who I visited in hospital, remember? He was the one who sent you the flowers and, if it has arrived, a hamper of goodies so we don't have to be bothered with cooking.'

Mrs Ward looked at her daughter curiously. 'Yes, I know who you are talking about – such a very generous man. I must write and thank him. You must tell me his address, dear.'

There was a slight pause, and then, as she started to lay the table for lunch, she glanced at Toni and asked: 'Have you heard from Justin? Last time we spoke on the phone, you said he hadn't been in touch for almost a week.'

Toni nodded. 'Yes, I had a text saying he's fine, and in case you think anything is wrong between us, Mother dear, you can think again. Justin is being incredibly patient, and if you think there's something going on between Aaron Osborn and me, I can assure you we are simply friends. It is possible to be friends with a man, you know! If you want the truth, I'm more sorry for Aaron than anything else. Not only did he lose his wife and nearly get killed himself trying to rescue her, but their friends have turned out to be her friends, not his, and he's terribly lonely.'

She proceeded to give her mother an account of Aaron's background and lack of family.

Mrs Ward was silent for a moment, then remarked: 'Well, be a little cautious, darling. He may just be a friend as far as you see it, but you are a very attractive young woman and if he's as lonely as you say, then . . .'

'Mum, you are miles off the mark,' Toni said. 'For one thing, Aaron showed me a photograph of his wife and I am very far from being his type. It isn't even a year since she died and of course he's still mourning her. We're just friends.'

'Your father and I were "just friends" before we fell in love,' Mrs Ward said. 'We'd both been invited to the same wedding. I was going out with a boy called Ronnie and your father was dating a girl called Sarah. We sat next to each other at the wedding lunch and next day we both wrote goodbye letters to our former dates and started going out with each other.'

Toni sighed. It was a story she'd heard many times from both parents, and she didn't for one moment doubt its veracity. It did not, however, have any relevance to her life. She loved Justin and they were going to be married. Maybe if she'd never met him or known he existed, she might have thought Aaron nice enough, attractive enough, to go out with him, even to have fallen for him, but nice as he was, it was Justin she loved. All she now prayed for was that her father would recover sufficiently for him to return home and she would be free to fly out and join Justin as soon as she possibly could.

FOURTEEN

The day before Toni was due to return to London, Julia telephoned her at Cherry Tree Cottage to say that Cynthia was not doing too badly as her PA, and she thought might improve her efficiency with more experience. Toni could, therefore, remain with her mother as long as she thought necessary. If Cynthia did prove herself to be adequately efficient, Toni would be free to join her boyfriend on the family cruise when her parents no longer needed her.

Glad as Toni was to hear that she did not have to hurry back to London while the prognosis for her father's recovery was still uncertain, she faced the fact that at the very best it could be several more weeks before she could hope to join Justin. His last email had said they had set off to cross the eastern end of the Mediterranean and had stopped at Cyprus before sailing on to Crete. The French family were staying with them as their twin offspring had just finished their university degrees and were enjoying a prolonged holiday together.

The twins, brother and sister, were really cool, Justin told her, and were proving to be good fun. Marisse, the daughter, was up for anything her twin Maurice did, such as skinny dipping off the yacht in the moonlight at three in the morning when they'd returned from an evening in a Larnaca nightclub, having spent the day scuba diving. She and Toni would get on like a house on fire, he maintained, and as the family were staying on board until they reached France, was there any hope she could join them before then?

Justin was not yet aware of her father's illness, as she had put off relaying the bad news of this further delay to her joining him. Now, at least with the encouraging news of Cynthia's progress, there was every hope she could join him soon. Meanwhile, he had the cheerful company of the French twins to make up for her absence, she told herself as she drove the car round to the front of the cottage where her mother was waiting impatiently to leave in good time for hospital visiting hours. Hopefully, they would find that her father had continued to show further signs of recovery. If so, she would set about finding an agency who could provide a retired nurse to come and look after him if her mother needed help when he was allowed home.

At least, by the sound of it, Justin was having a lot of fun and was clearly not missing her anything like as much as she was missing him. It was now almost twelve weeks since he and his parents had sailed out of Plymouth harbour, which meant she had already missed a quarter of the year-long cruise.

Driving along the now-familiar road to the hospital with her mother, Toni reflected that she would have felt much lonelier without Justin had it not been for the development of her friendship with Aaron Osborn. Aaron did not seem to mind how often she spoke of her long-term relationship with Justin and how much she was longing to join him. One of her old school friends who still lived in Bloxham had suggested that Aaron was playing a waiting game and was secretly in love with her, but Toni had laughed at the comment. Aaron had never made any untoward advances, she'd explained – never once tried to kiss her. In fact, on several different occasions, he had told her how much he valued their friendship.

Julia, too, had expressed doubts about such a friendship, especially as Toni had described Aaron as being a very attractive man, even admitting that she might have fallen for him if she'd not been in love with Justin. How come, Julia persisted, the guy professed to value Toni's friendship because he had so few other friends? Surely an attractive man in his late twenties who, so Toni had told her, was very well off, would have plenty of male and female friends to help him through his bereavement? What about the friends he and his late wife must have had?

Toni did her best to explain that Aaron was Scottish and differed in quite a few ways from his English contemporaries – which was hardly a valid explanation for his solitude, Julia argued. She did accept Toni's theory that the friends Aaron and his wife had as a married couple might have blamed him, an experienced skier, for not taking better care of his wife. But Toni was an extremely attractive girl and, unless this Scottish guy was blind, he couldn't be immune to that fact.

Julia, Toni had decided, was a bit old-fashioned, like her mother, in the conviction that opposite sexes could never have platonic friendships. It was true that Justin never saw a female without judging her feminine potential. He was instantly jealous of any male of whatever age who looked twice at her, but that seemed to Toni to be quite natural, seeing they'd been a couple for the best part of a year and were engaged to be married. She was jealous of the attractive young women who invariably milled around him at a party. Even now, she had to stop herself from feeling jealous that he was enjoying himself so much in the company of the amusing French girl called Marisse.

Toni's mood soared when, on reaching the hospital, she and her mother were told by the senior nurse that Mr Ward had now regained considerably more movement in his limbs. His speech, too, which had previously been too indistinct to understand, was now coherent. Smiling, she relayed the fact that on the doctor's visit that morning, he had been very pleased with Mr Ward's progress.

Mrs Ward was close to tears of relief as she hurried into the ward where her husband was lying.

The nurse turned to Toni and said gently, 'Don't let your mother expect that your father will automatically regain all his former abilities. He is noticeably better but we have no way of knowing when or how quickly these improvements might progress.'

Toni nodded. 'I understand, but my mother won't stop worrying until she has him home and can take care of him herself. I do realize that it's most unlikely she could manage to do so on her own as she is not physically very strong, but I intend to find someone – a retired nurse – who could live in and take care of them both. I have to go abroad, you see, so I won't be here to help them.'

The nurse nodded. 'When Mr Ward's doctor knows you have professional help for your father, I am sure he will allow Mr Ward to go home just as soon as he is assured that his condition has stabilized. Of course, he will need ongoing physiotherapy.'

She remained a moment or two longer, asking Toni where she was going on holiday, and having said how much she envied her a prolonged cruise on a private yacht, she hurried away to her other duties.

An hour later, as Toni drove her mother home, she listened to her euphoric chatter about all the improvements her beloved husband had made, and asked herself why she was having to make a conscious effort to share her mother's elation. Perhaps she was just tired: the anxiety of the past week had been quite a strain. Moreover, she had still been suffering from a minor recurrence of the food poisoning which had made her so ill in Spain. She now reached the conclusion that the generous portion of French mushroom paté from Aaron's food hamper had been responsible. The day after eating it, when she'd woken up, she'd felt distinctly queasy and was frequently sick. She now had to make an effort not to be irritated by her mother's repeated insistence that she would 'fade away' if she didn't eat 'properly'. As it was, she reiterated, Toni had not put back the weight she had lost in Spain.

'You must accept, my darling, that you have a weak constitution,' her mother said. 'Even as a little girl you were prone to car sickness if we drove more than a few miles!'

Turning the car into the familiar lane leading to Hook Norton village, Toni chided herself for being so self-absorbed. She had no reason to allow Justin's email to have an unsettling effect on her just because it highlighted what a wonderful and exciting time he was having without her. She should be pleased for him that he was having fun with the French twins and had omitted to say, as he usually did, how much he missed her. She had no valid excuse for depression now that it looked almost certain she would be able to join him in a few weeks' time.

Back in Cherry Tree Cottage, Joan Ward poured boiling water into the teapot and put two cups and saucers on the kitchen table, saying happily, 'I can hardly believe we may have Daddy home soon.' Her voice broke slightly as she continued: 'I was so afraid he would never come home! You have been such a help and comfort to me, my darling. I don't know how I would have got through this past week without you. I'll be able to manage when Daddy is back and then you can fly off and join that young man of yours.'

She opened a packet of Jaffa Cakes on to a plate and passed it to Toni. 'Your favourite, darling, so please don't tell me you don't want one.' She sat down and sipped her tea before adding: 'I'm so glad for you that that nice editor has found someone to take your place. You must be so relieved! Daddy was very proud of you, you know, when he heard you'd put your duty to her before your own pleasure. He said it was not every young person these days who would have delayed going on a cruise round the world the way you did. Which reminds me, Toni, before his stroke, when we first heard you were going to be gone for so long, Daddy said you mustn't worry about us whilst you are away as your Uncle James will always pop down and keep an eye on us if we need help.'

The uncle to whom her mother referred was Joan's elder brother, a bachelor who lived in Lancaster – not exactly a nearby village from which he could 'pop down', Toni had thought with a wry smile. Fortunately he would not be needed if there was a capable woman to look after her parents. Although still only in their sixties, both suffered from ill health – her mother with arthritis and her father from high blood pressure – so despite their denial that they needed an eye kept on them, Toni had always done exactly that. Hired help would be costly but they had their savings and she'd been told there would be an allowance of sorts from the council.

As she drank her tea and nibbled at a Jaffa Cake, Toni decided that she would not yet email Justin the news that she hoped shortly to be with him, although not until the tests showed her father was sufficiently recovered to be discharged.

That evening, as Toni and her mother sat watching *Midsomer Murders* on the television, Aaron called her on her mobile phone. He was at a loose end, he told her, and if she was not otherwise occupied at the weekend, he would enjoy a drive down to Hook Norton on the coming Sunday to take Toni and her mother out somewhere for lunch. London at the weekends on one's own was not much fun, he added, so it would be something pleasant for him to do.

Visiting times at the hospital did not start until three in the afternoons so there was no reason, Toni thought, why she and her mother could not go out to lunch with Aaron. Mrs Ward nodded her agreement, saying it would give her a chance to thank the kind man who had sent them the wonderful food hamper. She would be delighted to be taken out to lunch, provided they were back home in good time for the hospital visit.

Having told Aaron they would be pleased to see him, Toni found herself wondering if, on second thoughts, it was such a welcome plan. It would be nice to see him but, on the other hand, her digestive system had still not settled down, and although she had regained her appetite to some degree, she invariably felt nauseous after eating. If she agreed to go out for lunch, she would have to warn her mother on no account to mention the mushroom paté. Mrs Ward had wanted to write with a strong complaint to Harrods about the ill effects it had had on her daughter but, as Toni said, they had not been the purchasers, and the last thing she wanted was for Aaron to know his good deed had caused such a prolonged digestive upset.

Despite a day of almost continuous rain the day before, Sunday started with unbroken October sunshine. Mrs Ward arrived in Toni's bedroom with a cup of tea and, having drawn back the curtains, she asked anxiously: 'I can't make up my mind whether to wear my Marks and Spencer trouser suit or the maroon linen dress and jacket I wore on our wedding anniversary. What do you think is best, darling?'

Toni sat up in bed and drank a large mouthful of tea before replying gently. 'I don't think either would be quite right for a pub lunch, Mum. People just don't get dressed up these days – at least, not in the country. Why not wear your nice navy trousers and that flowery blouse – it goes with your fleece gilet. I'm wearing jeans and my puffa jacket.'

Mrs Ward looked doubtful. 'I'm sure you know best, darling, but won't your young man think we haven't bothered to look smart for him?'

'No, Mum!' Toni said, stifling a smile. 'He'll want us to look casual like everyone else. He won't be wearing a suit or a tie. And he is *not* "my young man". He's a friend – a very good and kind friend, but that's all. And in case you have forgotten me telling you, he knows all about Justin and that we're engaged to be married.'

She did not add, as she was tempted to do, that she and Justin would already be married if her parents had not been so anxious for them to wait until they'd known each other longer.

Aaron took them to The Gate Hangs High, a delightful pub in Hook Norton, where they enjoyed an excellent Sunday roast lunch at a table outside, enjoying the warmth of the autumn sunshine. Mrs Ward was as charmed by the way he looked after them both as she was by his unobtrusive good manners. In a very short while she lost all trace of shyness and was obviously flattered by the attention he paid her. She did notice that, every now and again, he would glance at Toni – an admiring glance which did not surprise her as her daughter was looking extremely pretty despite her pallor.

Towards the end of the meal she declined Aaron's suggestion of coffee on account of her imminent visit to the hospital. It was then that the thought suddenly struck her that this charming, caring man would have made Toni a far better husband than young Justin Metcalf. Not that she and her husband disliked Justin – it was just that he seemed to them to be more boy than adult, charming but not the kind of man who would make a responsible husband and father.

'Of course you mustn't be late, Mrs Ward!' Aaron was saying. 'Why don't I drive you direct to the hospital? It will save a lot of time if we don't have to go back to your house to get your car.'

Mrs Ward beamed and then her smile turned to a frown. 'But you'd have to wait for a whole hour before we went home!' she exclaimed. 'I'm sure if we hurry . . .'

'Really, I promise you I don't mind waiting,' Aaron interrupted. 'If Toni is not intending to see her father, maybe we could go for a walk. I am sure there are some good walks nearby and the trees are such a wonderful colour at this time of year.' He looked expectantly at Toni.

Her first reaction was to decline the suggestion, but it then occurred to her that maybe her mother would like her father's undivided attention for the brief hour's visiting time. She smiled at Aaron, impressed by his thoughtfulness, and happily let him hold her hand as they walked towards his car. When they arrived at the hospital they watched her mother disappear as she hurried impatiently down one of the long corridors toward the cardiac ward.

'I'm struck by your parents' devotion to one another,' he said as he tucked his hand under her arm and led her back outside into the October sunshine. Although the wind was getting cold it was still a lovely afternoon, the sun highlighting the beautiful colours of the autumn leaves on the trees and underfoot in the hospital grounds.

Toni drew in lungfuls of crisp cold air and felt a sudden lift of her spirits. Smiling up at him, she said, 'Mum spoke to Dad's doctor this morning and he said that, unless anything goes very wrong, which he is not expecting to happen, my father will be allowed home next week or the week after. So if I can get a competent retired nurse or the like to look after them it looks as if at long last I shall be able to fly out and join Justin.'

Unaware of the look of dismay clouding Aaron's handsome face, she continued: 'He told me the *Silver Sprite*, their yacht, will be stopping in France at Nice, so if I can book a flight to Nice it will be perfect.'

'You haven't booked a flight yet?'

Toni shook her head. 'No, I don't want to tempt Fate. Justin said they will be staying in Nice for at least a week, so I'm sure I'll get a seat – if not on British Airways then on one of the other airlines.'

For a moment or two, Aaron did not speak. When he did so, he was unable to control the emotion in his voice. 'I can't pretend that news is welcome. I'm going to miss you, Toni! Very much. You have become a very dear friend.' His voice thickened. 'Ever since you first came to my bedside in the Carlos Haya Hospital and I saw the compassion in your eyes, I realized you were someone very special . . .' He broke off, turning his head away so she could no longer see his face. 'Please don't think I am not fully aware of your love for the man you expect to marry. I have always known that, but . . . well, it did cross my mind that things might not work out as you hoped.'

Colour flooded Toni's face as Aaron's words forced her to recognize the fact that, for his part, their friendship was not as platonic as she had led herself to believe. She was not only disturbed by the realization, but guilty. She should have realized that his anxiety always to see her and fall in with her plans, seemingly without any of his own, was not just the result of his loneliness and his sadness at his wife's death. She had told herself that he needed an understanding friend just as she needed his sympathy and support whilst she had so many problems to deal with. If Justin had been at home, he would have been the person she'd have gone to with her concerns.

She was now tongue-tied, uncertain whether to refer to her concerns about his feelings. Perhaps, she told herself, it was better not to do so. In a few weeks' time she would be on her way to France and Aaron would know that it was Justin who had her heart. Hoping to emphasize the fact, she said brightly, 'I can't wait for Dad's doctor to confirm when he can definitely go home. Then I can book my flight and text Justin to say I'm finally on my way. I've missed him so much!' She attempted a smile at Aaron's rigid face. 'If it hadn't been for you, I don't know what I would have done. You've been such a very good friend to me, Aaron.'

For a full sixty seconds, Aaron did not speak. When he did so, his voice was tightly controlled. 'I think we should be going back to the hospital. We must have been gone more than an hour and your mother will be waiting.'

Nevertheless, Toni felt uneasy when Aaron did not reach out to tuck her arm under his as they retraced their steps. The omission made her even more certain that he had been concealing a burgeoning affection for her.

FIFTEEN

Only when the sign to fasten seat belts ready for landing went up above Toni's head did she allow herself to give way to the overwhelming feeling of excitement. In a matter of minutes she would see Justin waiting for her at the barrier outside Customs. It had been fifteen weeks since she had last seen him. They had not parted on the best of terms, Justin having refused to accept that she could not simply give in her notice without allowing Julia time to find a suitable replacement for her. When would they ever again have the chance of a world cruise together? he'd said again and again. Toni was always saying what a nice, kind, understanding person Julia was – surely she would let Toni go? He had not understood that it was because of Julia's good nature that Toni was not prepared to leave her without a replacement. 'You care more about her than you do about me!' Justin had said childishly.

His texts to her after he had departed with his parents were more brief accounts of the yacht's itinerary than loving messages. Lately, his frequent references to the French twins and the fun they were having were, she was sure, partly to make her regret her decision not to go with him. All that had changed when she'd finally been able to tell him that at last she was free to join him. Only then were his texts filled with ardent messages of love – of how much he'd missed her; how he was counting the hours to her arrival. The texts had arrived almost hourly.

For a fleeting moment, as the plane touched down on the runway, Toni thought of Aaron's expression as he had waved her through security at Heathrow Airport. He had not attempted to kiss her goodbye. All he'd said was, 'Keep in touch, Toni! I'm going to miss you. Don't forget that I'm always available if ever you need a friend.'

Might she need him? She thought of the weeks of continuing bouts of sickness, during which she had tried to convince herself that it did not necessarily mean she was pregnant. It was two months since the nausea had started and now not only were her breasts noticeably bigger but so too was her stomach. Justin would be blind not to notice these changes – she would have to enlighten him to the truth. The thought of whether he would be pleased plagued her day and night. She had no choice but to tell him now, but she was very far from sure he would want to become a father.

Everything depended upon whether he still loved her or whether the past fifteen weeks of separation had caused him to change his mind.

It was the longest time they had been apart. Would things have changed? Had he discovered that the French girl, Marisse, who he'd mentioned several times, was more fun to be with than she was? Aaron's farewell remark was no doubt intended to be reassuring. He would be there to pick up the pieces, he'd told her, as if he was expecting that Justin might not still love her as much as ever – or worse still, not at all.

Justin's texts had been quite open about his friendship with the French twins. The family had joined the *Silver Sprite* at the mouth of the Suez Canal and sailed up to Port Said with them. However, instead of disembarking at Port Said, where they were intending to fly back to France, they had stayed on the yacht to enjoy the Metcalfs' planned visits to Cyprus, Crete, Sicily and Sardinia before arriving at Nice, which was where Toni was about to join them. With their companionship and such an exciting itinerary to enjoy, would Justin have had time to miss her?

Such qualms vanished as she waited for her luggage to come round on the airport carousel and thought of the fashionable new clothes she had bought regardless of the cost. All were entirely suitable for a cruise but loose enough to be comfortable later on in her pregnancy.

She put her irrational worries to the back of her mind. Justin's texts may have been short of endearments and confined to geographical descriptions of the places he had visited, but they had never failed to end with 'LYL4A', their personal shorthand for *Love You Lots For Always* – something he had devised on one of the occasions when he was being endearingly childish. It was now habitual for them both to use the letters in place of their names at the end of their texts.

Toni now recalled Justin's last text saying they had left Sardinia and were about to dock in Nice harbour. He couldn't wait to meet her at the airport the next day. The text ended as always with their code and all Toni's qualms suddenly vanished. She had no more reason to doubt his love than he had to doubt hers, she reminded herself.

Her thoughts turned to Mr and Mrs Metcalf's plan, which was to take them from France down the eastern coast of Spain, through the Straits of Gibraltar and across the Atlantic to the Caribbean. She hoped Justin's mother, who always looked so fashionably dressed, would approve of her new clothes.

There was a sudden stir amongst the waiting passengers as the first pieces of luggage started to appear on the carousel. Toni waited impatiently for her case, knowing it was only a few more minutes until she would be in Justin's arms. There was a brief delay until it finally appeared. She passed unhindered through Customs, her heart beating with excited anticipation as she caught sight of Justin waving to her.

Conscious only of her joy at seeing him, Toni did not immediately notice the pretty blonde girl standing next to him.

His face lit up in a wide smile as he hurried to her side and bent his head and kissed her. 'Thought your plane was never going to get here!' he said. Then, holding her a little apart from him, he added: 'You're looking wonderful but your face looks thinner. You've lost weight, haven't you, darling?'

Realizing that he could not have noticed her thickened waistline, she was trying to think of a suitable reply when he turned to the blonde girl in a brightly coloured maxi sundress at his side.

'We'll have to fatten Toni up, won't we, Marisse?' He turned back to Toni and, smiling apologetically, said, 'I should have introduced you. Marisse, meet my Toni, who you've heard so much about.'

With an effort to hide her disappointment that Justin had not come to greet her on his own, Toni tried to find something suitable to say, but the very last thing was *I'm so pleased to meet you!* as she most certainly was not. She had imagined her reunion with Justin would be just the two of them.

As if aware of her thoughts, Justin said awkwardly, 'Let's get out of here, shall we? I really hate airports: too many people milling around like flocks of lost sheep. But Marisse loves them, don't you, babe, and she was determined to come with me to meet you.' Looking slightly flustered, he took Toni's suitcase and led the way across the concourse to the Exit sign.

'You two wait here whilst I go and get the car,' he said. 'Hopefully I won't be too long.'

It was not until Justin was out of sight that either girl spoke. Then Marisse said in her attractive broken accent: 'It is so good to meet you, Toni.' She pronounced her name 'Tonee'. 'Justin tells me you are his very good friend and that you and I will like each other for company.' Without waiting for a reply, she continued: 'As you can imagine, it has been so happy a time for me on the boat always to have his attention.' Her eyes narrowed and she gave a strange little laugh. 'When Justin tells me you are coming to be with us, I said he must not have concern – that we will share him until you go home.'

'But I have no intention of going home!' Toni said, controlling her tone of voice with difficulty. 'Nor of "sharing" Justin, as you put it. Didn't he tell you that we are engaged to be married?'

The French girl seemed unfazed by this remark. Smiling, she replied sweetly: '*Bien sur*, most certain he has told me this. I ask him why you do not marry now and he tells me that your parents have fear you and Justin are not truly *compatible*. Is that not so?'

Toni's euphoric mood now vanished completely as she asked herself if the French girl imagined that her relationship with Justin was a trial one or, worse still, that Justin now considered it to be so. Had he been comparing her with Marisse, discovering whether she was a better lover? Had he been unfaithful to her? Without warning, it flashed through her mind that he and the French girl had now had several weeks together in close proximity on the yacht, and everything the girl had said implied a degree of intimacy. Was it possible her unexpected announcement that she was free at last to join him had been an embarrassment to Justin? If so, why had he not told her he'd grown tired of waiting for her and was involved with someone else?

An hour later, Toni was still feeling far from celebrating as Justin took her hand and led her up on to the deck of the *Silver*

Sprite. Mr and Mrs Metcalf were waiting to greet her, as was Marisse's twin, Maurice. Her arrival had coincided with a steward's announcement that lunch was ready, so there was only time for Justin to take her and her suitcase to his cabin and for her to freshen her make-up and tidy her hair before they hurried into the salon.

An elaborate cold buffet lunch awaited them. A large lobster nestled in a crisp green lettuce in the centre of the table, huge Mediterranean prawns encircling it. Two delicious salads lay either side of it and there was a tempting array of oysters on a plate of crushed ice, with avocados and hors d'oeuvres on a side table.

'We have got to put back some weight on Toni,' Justin said solicitously as he sat down beside her, with Marisse promptly sitting down on his other side. He heaped a plate of food and put it down in front of Toni. 'I expect you to eat all that, hon!'

He was looking at her so lovingly that Toni felt tears of confusion filling her eyes. She stood up abruptly and asked Mrs Metcalf to excuse her, saying truthfully that the flight had left her a bit nauseous.

Justin jumped up and took her arm. 'You can have a lie down this afternoon,' he said solicitously, 'and then you will feel up to this evening's outing. Monsieur and Madame Bourget will have returned from their visit to Monte Carlo by then and have plans for us all. They are taking us to Le Bar des Oiseaux for dinner – it's one of their cabaret nights. Afterwards, there's a nightclub the twins and I thought we'd go on to for some dancing, so it could be a late night.'

It was only with a huge effort that Toni managed not to say that she didn't feel like any kind of celebration until she was reassured about his relationship with the French girl. When they reached his cabin, before she could speak, Justin sat down on the bed beside her and drew her into his arms, kissed her mouth, her eyes, her cheeks and her throat hungrily.

'God, how I've missed you!' he said huskily as he smoothed her hair back from her forehead. 'I've wanted to do this ever since I saw you walking towards us at the airport.' He kissed her again. 'I didn't want Marisse to come with me but . . . well, she insisted.' He gave a sudden devastating smile, adding: 'Perhaps it was just as well she did or I might have made love to you there and then!'

Misty-eyed, Toni drew away and, no longer able to restrain herself, said impetuously: 'When I saw you with Marisse I thought perhaps you and she . . .' She broke off uncertainly.

Justin was now smiling. 'So that's what was bothering you! No, my darling, take my word for it, there's nothing going on between me and Marisse. She *is* very flirtatious and I dare say if it weren't for the way I feel about you, I might have been tempted. Her twin, Maurice, once told me to ignore her come-ons, that it's just the way she behaves with any man she fancies. He is devoted to her, but that doesn't stop him calling her the world's worst *coquette*.'

His face became serious suddenly as he pushed her gently back against the pillows.

'Are you still feeling off colour, Toni? I so much want to make love to you, but . . .'

Reassured by Justin's description of Marisse, Toni reached up and wound her arms round his neck. This was not the time to tell him about the baby, she thought as he covered her face with kisses once more. She would do that later – tonight, perhaps, when they were alone in bed together and had time to talk uninterrupted.

'I've missed you so much!' she whispered. 'And I'm not ill – it's just a passing feeling of nausea I've been getting from time to time. It isn't serious.'

Justin needed no further reassurance. As his mouth devoured hers and his hands reached under her T-shirt, there was a sharp knock on the door. Justin was on the point of calling out to whoever it was to go away as he didn't wish to be disturbed, when the door opened and Marisse stepped inside.

She was holding a large dessert plate of fruit which she now placed on the table beside Toni. Not seeming shocked or even surprised to see the couple on the bed, even as Toni hastily pulled down her T-shirt, she said brightly in her accented English: 'I noticed that you had not eaten when you left the table, Tonee, so I have brought you these.' She pointed to the plate so Toni could see the bunches of green and black grapes, the peach and greengages surrounded by strawberries. 'Madame Metcalf said it is important that you eat.'

Feeling both embarrassed and annoyed by the girl's untimely entrance, Toni did no more than nod her thanks, but Marisse had already turned her attention to Justin.

'Maurice has requested you tell him, *chéri*, if you intend to go water-skiing with him this afternoon. He has done as you requested and booked a time for three o'clock.'

It was a split second before Justin said hurriedly, 'Surely Maurice realized that with Toni arriving today I would not be going anywhere? The two of you can enjoy yourselves without me.'

Her mouth pouting, Marisse shrugged, allowing the strap of her maxi dress to slip halfway down her arm.

'But, *chéri*, you know how I am always needing you to give me the confidence,' she murmured.

Justin was unsmiling as, ignoring her comment, he replied: 'You'd better go and make my apologies to Maurice . . . I'm sure the two of you will have a good afternoon's sport without me!'

Ignoring Marisse's pout, Justin got off the bed and all but pushed her out of the cabin, locking the door after her. Returning to the bedside, he remarked, 'I suppose it never crossed her mind that we were about to make love.'

Toni was about to question Marisse's innocence, but Justin was undressing her, kissing every part of her body as he exposed it, and she forgot Marisse as she helped him out of his T-shirt and shorts.

'I had forgotten how beautiful you are!' Justin exclaimed as he caressed her breasts. 'God, Toni, I can't count the number of nights I've lain awake thinking of the times we made love and how special it always was. I've missed you so, so much,' he added huskily.

He kicked back the duvet, which was impeding his movements, and lowered his body on to hers. Toni's legs parted to accommodate him, her hands pulling him as tightly as possible against her body as he thrust inside her.

'Love you, love you, love you!' he murmured huskily each time he thrust into her. They climaxed almost simultaneously. Lying quietly beside Justin, only their hurried breathing breaking the silence, Toni decided that this was the most wonderful of all the times they had made love. Perhaps it was because, having been apart for so long, it was as if they had lost each other and this had been a magical reuniting.

For several minutes, neither of them spoke. Then Justin leaned on one elbow and, looking down at her lovingly, said, 'I think we could do with a bottle of bubbly to celebrate your arrival after all this time.' He got out of bed and pulled on his shorts. 'Stay where you are, babe. You look so comfortable there! I'll be as quick as I can.'

For a minute or two after he had gone, Toni wondered how she could ever have doubted Justin's love for her, still less hers for him. They belonged together, and she was never, ever going to be parted from him again.

The yacht had been moored in the harbour, so as there were no rough seas to worry about, the porthole in their cabin was ajar and a slight breeze was wafting through it, cooling Toni's hot, naked body. She sat up and reached down to pull up the duvet from the bottom of the bed. As she did so, her eye was caught by something coloured fuchsia pink that was partly concealed by the duvet. Curious to know what it could be, she leaned over and pulled it out.

For a moment, she could not think what it was, and then she identified the bottom half of a woman's bikini. She sat still, staring at it stupidly. How could such a garment possibly find its way down beneath the duvet to the foot of Justin's bed? Had Justin not seen it there? Obviously it was not his!

Like a sharp pain in her solar plexus, Toni guessed at once to whom it belonged. Justin's mother, Mrs Metcalf, was highly unlikely to wear such a skimpy object of apparel and, even if she did, how could it possibly have found its way into Justin's bed? Toni now felt a wave of sickness as the truth engulfed her. It could only belong to Marisse.

SIXTEEN

With an effort, Toni tried to disprove her suspicion, but she knew in her heart that, since her arrival at the airport, the French girl had never been less than proprietorial. She behaved as if Justin belonged to her and Toni was no more than an old flame who must be got rid of. Toni had never imagined that Justin would have the French girl with him when he met her at the airport. Seeing Marisse had not been a pleasure but she'd quickly told herself that some people saw such hugely busy places as exciting, even glamorous, and it may have been for that reason that Marisse had wanted to accompany Justin.

Nevertheless, by the time he had driven them to the harbour in the hired car, the French girl's proprietorial manner over Justin had become unmistakeable. So, too, was his embarrassment as he had pretended to ignore it each time Marisse had called him *chéri*.

Her heart jolted as she heard Justin's footsteps outside the cabin door. Springing out of bed, she pulled on her bra and knickers and quickly slipped on her T-shirt as he came into the room. He stopped in his tracks and stared at her incredulously.

'What's up, hon?' he asked as he put down the tray he was carrying. 'I thought . . .' He broke off as his eye caught sight of Marisse's bikini lying on top of the sheet.

His first reaction was one of disbelief. 'Wherever did that come from?' he asked, frowning. 'Marisse must have dropped it on the bed when we got back from wind surfing yesterday. She and Maurice joined me here for drink . . .' He broke off and looked anxiously at Toni. 'Hey, hon, you weren't thinking that Marisse had been in my bed and . . .'

He broke off once more as he realized from Toni's expression that this was exactly the conclusion she had reached. With an effort, she was struggling to choke back the threatening tears as she closed the zip of her skirt.

Controlling her voice, she said, 'I'd like to believe that, but I don't, Justin.' She held the thong between her thumb and finger. 'I don't think this was "dropped" underneath your duvet yesterday. For one thing, surely you or the steward would have seen it when the bed was made this morning.' Her voice hardened. 'You know as well as I do that when we've been in a hurry to make love, we've taken off our clothes and kicked them out of the way. When you and I . . .' She broke off, unable to trust her voice any longer.

Justin was standing white-faced, looking directly into Toni's eyes as he said emphatically: 'I give you my word that I have never made love to Marisse. I'd be silly to pretend that there weren't odd times when I was tempted, and I admit I have kissed the girl on the odd occasion, but she has known from the start that you and I are engaged, and that we would be getting married next year.'

He sounded so sincere, so plausible, that Toni now hesitated before reaching a final conclusion. In a carefully controlled voice, she said, 'I'm doing my best to believe you, Justin. This,' she held up the bikini thong again, 'was a bit of a shock. Frankly I am finding it a little hard to cast Marisse as the innocent little girl who thinks it is a joke to leave her bikini bottoms in a man's bed. Don't you agree, Justin?'

Justin's voice hardened. Ignoring her question, he said, 'You seem determined to believe the worst of her and of me despite my giving you my word that nothing serious has ever happened between us. Why can't you believe me?' He drew a deep breath before adding: 'I've been counting the hours until I saw you at the airport. I dreamed about our reunion and how it would be, and now . . .' He stopped mid-sentence, his voice breaking.

Could she believe him? He'd admitted to kissing the French girl, but that was no big deal. Although she had never kissed Aaron, she had enjoyed a very close friendship with him. It would have been unnatural for Justin not to enjoy in her absence a flirtation with a young, pretty girl who fancied him, but not to enjoy a sexual relationship when he was engaged to marry her. Her instincts told her that Marisse was very far from being the flirtatious little girl she pretended to be. Nor did she doubt, although she could not have proved it, that Marisse was in love with Justin.

Toni now decided that Marisse was determined to have him as her lover . . . if she had not already achieved it. Quite suddenly, it crossed her mind that it was just possible that Marisse had deliberately put her bikini under Justin's duvet in order to bring about the present discord between them.

Justin's expression of surprise and dismay now gave way to one of anger. This was exacerbated by the memory of how often in the past few weeks he had come close to submitting to Marisse's very frank demands that they should be making the most of their opportunities to include sex in their relationship. Even when he had had too much to drink, he had stayed faithful to Toni, confining himself with difficulty to the passionate exchange of kisses which Marisse had instigated. He had resolutely resisted her overt temptations for sex. They had become so intense he'd finally been obliged to threaten to veto any time alone with her unless she accepted that he was very much in love with Toni and would never be unfaithful to her.

Now, Toni's disbelief in his innocence seemed grossly unfair. Admittedly, the wretched bikini appearing in his bed was odd to say the least and bound to arouse suspicion but, try as he might, he could not explain how it had got there unless Marisse had put it there – and he suspected that she had done it deliberately in order to achieve exactly what had now happened. It was not surprising that Toni had reached the intended conclusion.

Quietly, he repeated again: 'You have my word I have never had sex with Marisse, although I have admitted I did on occasions kiss her. Remember our promise, Toni, that we would always trust each other to tell the truth? So why won't you believe what I am telling you?' His voice suddenly hardened. 'It's your concern, not mine, if you can't believe me. Maybe you are just overtired or overwrought or something. You don't look well, so I suggest you get back into bed and have some rest. I'll cancel tonight's outing. Meanwhile, I've quite a few things to see to on deck. I'll come back later when I hope you'll be feeling a lot better.' Without so much as looking at her, he turned and left the cabin.

For a few moments, Toni remained motionless, her mind

whirling and a distressing feeling of nausea overcoming her. She had been mercifully free of the ongoing bouts of nausea that had occurred until several weeks ago. Only once as the aeroplane was coming in to land had she felt in the least bit sick. Now, as she found her way into the en-suite bathroom and her stomach was emptying itself, she was reminded of her pregnancy, and that she had still not told Justin they were expecting a baby.

Returning to the cabin, she lay down on the bed and, leaning back against the pillows, tried to work out how she'd come to be pregnant. She recalled the last time that she and Justin had made love, the night before he had left to join his parents on board the *Silver Sprite*. The previous week she had not renewed her prescription for the pill, knowing she would not need it while they were apart. That last night, Justin had no alternative means of birth control, and they'd agreed that it couldn't possibly matter this once . . .

Toni closed her eyes, certain that this was how and when she had conceived. Dry-eyed, she asked herself if Justin could be right when he'd said she was probably overtired and overwrought, jumping to unfair conclusions about his relationship with Marisse. Should she have trusted him not to lie to her?

Toni now tried to find other explanations for the bikini. Was it possible that Marisse might have come to Justin's cabin with her twin after a swim, put her swimming gear at the foot of the bed and forgotten about it when she left? Justin had looked and sounded innocent, and the very least she could do was give him the benefit of the doubt. He was the least devious person she knew, and it was that frankness that had first attracted her to him.

Her thoughts now went to the baby in her womb. How would Justin feel about it? If they resolved this present problem, would they get married at once? Or would he be horrified at the idea of becoming a father? It would be a huge shock to him, as indeed it had been to her.

Suddenly she knew what she must do – what she wanted to do. When Justin returned to the cabin, she would tell him she was sorry not to have trusted him; that it was because she loved him so much that she had been jealous of the pretty French girl who had spoiled their reunion. When he had forgiven her, then she would tell him that he was going to be a father.

Toni was now overcome by impatience as she lay silently listening for his footsteps approaching the cabin door. It was not Justin's steps she heard, however, but those of Marisse, who had seen Justin leaving the room and grabbed the opportunity to see Toni on her own.

SEVENTEEN

Aaron stood at the window of the sitting room in his London flat looking over the tree tops on Clapham Common. He had chosen this fourth-floor apartment as much for the spectacular view as for its convenience for getting into central London. On the table beside him was his computer and a half-finished letter to his insurance company who were refusing to pay his claim for his and Leena's skis lost in the accident.

After Toni had left the country to meet up with her boyfriend, he had been trying unsuccessfully to find something to do with his time. He had no wish to return to his law studies now that he was a rich man, but he knew he must try to find a way to put Toni out of his mind. For the first time in his life, he realized, he had fallen in love, but with a girl beyond his reach.

He no longer tried to pretend otherwise as he identified the emotion he had never felt before. Any love he might have had initially for his parents had been swiftly eroded by their obvious disinterest in him. He had been a solitary little boy, conversing only with their Japanese servants. At his prep school in England he had been teased and ridiculed for his difference from the other small boys who nicknamed him 'Mikado' because of his constant references to the Japanese way of life. At his public school he had been very much a loner, his reticence making it impossible for him to join in the usual student levity. As for the female undergraduates at university, he was too shy to take advantage of their open approval of his good looks.

It had not been until he'd met Leena, with her undisguised passion for him, that he began to appreciate the enormous advantages of his sex appeal. Her unbridled passion which dominated their sexual encounters was always followed by extravagant presents for him from expensive men's outfitters. His uncle's meagre allowance had only ever enabled him to buy the cheapest ready-made clothes and shoes. Leena's presents transformed him. He now had stunning cashmere sweaters, a Patek Philippe watch,

an assortment of Ralph Lauren ties, gold cufflinks from Asprey's
and a Russian leather wallet. Leena had been nothing if not
generous, even before their marriage. Now, of course, he could
continue to lead the life she'd taught him to take for granted.

Sighing as he recalled those years, Aaron returned to his
computer, thinking that even then the only strong emotion he had
ever experienced was not love but dislike – dislike for his parents,
his teachers, his youthful tormentors and not least his uncle, who
he'd known to be a fairly wealthy man, but who'd kept his
allowance to the absolute minimum.

His mouth tightened, distorting his good looks. How deeply
he had resented that strange, dour Scotsman's control of his life;
the rules he'd laid down, so rigid that even the slightest trans-
gression had elicited a thrashing – the degree of force depending
upon the severity of Aaron's misbehaviour. How he had longed
to be tall and strong enough to defend himself, to hit back, but at
the end of the day, he was only too aware that the man he hated
was also the man who provided a home of sorts and paid reluctantly for his education. That youthful dislike turned to hatred
when his uncle died suddenly, and left every penny he had to
the British Legion.

If he ever wrote a book, he would make his uncle the victim
in a murder story. Destroying him fictionally was the only way
he could exact his revenge.

Before he could complete the letter he had left unfinished, his
telephone rang. It rang very seldom and so he answered it with
some curiosity. To his incredulity, it was Toni's mother, Mrs
Ward. She sounded quite agitated as she spoke, close to tears.

'Oh, Mr Osborn, I'm so glad I've got you. I wasn't sure if I
had the right number.' Without waiting for him to speak, she
hurried on, saying, 'I've just had a telephone call from Toni.
She's coming home and will be arriving at Gatwick at four
o'clock tomorrow afternoon. She wants me to arrange for a taxi
to meet her and drive her down here, but . . .'

At this point she broke off, and Aaron realized that she was trying
to control tears. His own heart was beating with excitement.

'There's no need for you to arrange a taxi; I will meet Toni,'
he said quickly. 'Did she tell you her flight number, Mrs Ward?
Not that I need it if she is coming from Nice. I'll find her.'

There followed a volume of tearful thanks from Mrs Ward. She was so worried, she told Aaron tremulously. Toni had only been out in France for a few hours when she phoned home, but hadn't said what had gone wrong. She'd promised to explain everything when she got home but she'd sounded as if . . . she was crying.

At this point, Mrs Ward began to apologize. 'I shouldn't be bothering you, Mr Osborn, but you've been so very kind in the past, taking us out to lunch and driving me to the hospital and the flowers and everything . . .'

Here was Aaron's chance to interrupt. 'Mrs Ward, I do assure you it was my pleasure to be of help. As for meeting your daughter off the plane, I will be only too pleased to do so. Toni was extremely kind to me when I had my accident in Spain so I am more than happy to have this chance to help her in any way I can, and I will enjoy the drive down to you tomorrow. I could offer her a room here in London but I imagine she is anxious to be with you.'

'So thoughtful of you, Mr Osborn!' Mrs Ward drew an audible sigh. 'I didn't think Toni was feeling very well when she left us, and if she's ill I can look after her here. My husband is improving every day and I have a wonderful ex-nurse who takes care of everything.'

She paused once more but only briefly before adding: 'When Toni told me to order a taxi for her, I was worried she might not have enough money to pay for it to bring her all the way here, and I didn't want her taking a train to Banbury and having to change stations with her luggage and everything.'

'You can rely on my bringing her safely home, Mrs Ward,' Aaron said reassuringly. 'It's absolutely no trouble, I do assure you, and I'm just so pleased you have rung me. Please try not to worry: I'm sure everything will be all right. Possibly if Toni hasn't been feeling well, she just wants to be home with her mother.'

Mrs Ward jumped on the suggestion. 'Yes, you're probably right, Mr Osborn. Toni never really recovered fully from that bout of food poisoning she had a few months ago in Spain. I did suggest she postponed her departure to France but she wouldn't consider it: said she'd been waiting far too long already to join

her young man.' She gave a deep sigh. 'I suppose it isn't for me
to say but I didn't think it was right for him to go away without
her.' She broke off as she remembered that she was talking to
someone who was almost a stranger.

It was on the tip of Aaron's tongue to say that Mrs Ward's
comment very closely reflected his own. Why had Justin Metcalf
not postponed his holiday in order to be with the girl he supposedly loved? Toni had not hidden the fact from him that she'd
been desperately anxious to be reunited with the man to whom
she was engaged. Was it possible that when their reunion had
finally happened, it had not lived up to expectations?

Having reassured Mrs Ward once more that he would be sure
to meet Toni's plane, he replaced the phone on its rest and went
once more to the window. His heart was racing as he reviewed
the unexpected turn of events. Not a few minutes ago he had
been filled with depression at the thought of the days to come
without his meetings with Toni to look forward to. Her father's
illness had played into his hands, delaying her departure still
further after she had been replaced at her office. She had needed
his help, and in giving it, she had come to look on him as a very
close friend, confiding in him – trusting him completely.

Was it possible, he asked himself as he watched the stream of
cars crossing the common on their way to and from the city, that
Fate was playing into his hands? That Toni and her boyfriend
had quarrelled so seriously that she had simply turned round and
was heading home on her own?

His mind raced. If there had been a quarrel – a serious one
– he would be there to offer consolation, sympathy, companionship and, when the time was right, his love.

Excited by his thoughts, Aaron knew he could not finish the
letter he was writing. Instead, he went to his desk and pulled out
a notepad. Sitting down, he started to write a list of things he
wished to buy before he met Toni the next day. First was a
sweetener for Mrs Ward – an orchid, perhaps, a white one. She'd
like that. Next, a book for Mr Ward – *Golf Courses of the World*,
perhaps? The old boy had been a keen golfer in his day. Then
something for Toni herself. He'd love to buy her a bottle of
Cartier's Panthère, the expensive scent Leena had always referred
to as the most exquisite in the world, but his instincts warned

him to think of something less ostentatious. He decided to visit Harrods perfume department where he selected Amitié. Reasonably priced, it was a present one friend might bestow upon another with no amorous implications. He knew instinctively that it was far too soon for him to be revealing his love.

In the taxi back to his flat, Aaron's head was high and there was a hint of a smile on his face. He was happy – happy for the first time since Toni had announced the date she was leaving England and he had not known when he would see her again, believing as he did that her reunion with Metcalf was the death knell to any hopes that she might one day turn to him.

Aaron might have been even more ecstatic had he known that at least the first part of his conjectures had already happened, and that Toni had told Justin that she never wanted to see him again.

Toni was sitting dry-eyed at the window of her hotel bedroom near Nice Airport. Looking at her watch, she saw that it was less than two hours since she and Justin had been making love in his cabin on the yacht and then Marisse had shattered that dream. Somehow she had managed to keep the renewed feelings of nausea at bay until after the taxi had driven her from the *Silver Sprite* and deposited her here at one of the hotels overlooking the airport. Not only was she feeling physically ill but also emotionally exhausted.

It was small comfort that she had not told Justin she was pregnant. It had been difficult enough making him believe that she no longer loved him and intended to go home. Finally, despite his desperate protests, she had stormed out of the cabin. Justin had not been on deck to watch her leave.

At least Marisse had been honest – painfully honest – confessing that she and Justin had been having a light-hearted affair almost from the day she had come on board. They were words Toni would never forget. Angry tears stung her eyes as she recalled the sight of Marisse's pretty face when, sitting on the end of the bed, she had apologized for – of all things – her untidiness.

'Justin is quite right to be so angry with me,' she said. 'I promised him when we heard you were finally arriving here that

I would make sure everything belonging to me would be removed before you came. But you should not be angry with him. It is you he loves, and he has never pretended to me otherwise. At first, he refused to make love to me, telling me he wished to remain faithful to you, but . . .'

She had broken off and dabbed at her large blue eyes with a tissue. 'I did not let myself fall in love with Justin although it would have been so easy to do so. He is quite charming and . . . well, we were both lonely and it was not truly an affair . . . just sex between two lonely people who liked each other. You do understand, don't you, *chérie*?'

Oh, yes, she had understood all right, Toni told herself bitterly. Unbelievably, the French girl seemed to think that a sexual relationship with another woman's fiancé was quite normal, acceptable. Justin on the other hand had tried to hide the truth, which proved his conscience was far from clear. Marisse's excuse that they had been lonely was in no way acceptable.

Toni's eyes filled once more with tears as she reflected that it was several months since he had last made love to her, but what kind of excuse was that? Was she expecting too much of him to be faithful? If, after they were married, they were obliged to spend time apart, would that be a licence to have an affair? To go to bed with someone you'd just met? How could she ever trust him? What might happen when he was on one of his week-long golfing holidays with his friends? Did girls go with them? Or did they pick up any girls who happened to be around?

Marisse's protestations had become more forceful. She was the guilty one, she repeated: it was she who had gone naked to Justin's cabin and offered herself, put temptation in his way – she was the one who should now leave the yacht, not Toni.

At this point, tears slid down the girl's cheeks. '*Mes parents!* They will never forgive me. They have been so happy with Monsieur and Madame Metcalf. Maurice, too. So you see, Toni, I will be punished for my wrong doing and Justin will no longer be angry with me, and you and he will—'

'No!' Toni had all but shouted the word. 'No, you don't understand. If Justin had really loved me . . .' Unable to continue, she had said as firmly as she could manage: 'My mind is made up: I shall go home. Please be good enough to telephone for a

---

taxi to take me to the airport, and tell Justin I don't wish to see him. We have nothing to say to each other, and I shan't change my mind.'

Her departure was a bit of a blur: Justin pleading with her, Mr and Mrs Metcalf trying to persuade her not to make any decisions in a hurry – that whatever had happened could be put right. As if in a bad dream, she had been driven through the busy streets to the airport, booked a flight home for the following morning, and booked herself into the hotel. Vaguely, she recalled that she'd been certain the taxi driver had overcharged her, but she didn't care. Finally, she had been able to phone home from the telephone in her hotel bedroom.

Her call to her mother had been brief, telling her only that she had decided to come home. Now she clung to that word – home. Home, where she could lie down in her own bed in her own childhood bedroom, pull the covers over her head and block out the world.

In less than twenty-four hours she would be safe, she thought. Her poor mother had sounded distraught on the telephone, worrying as she always did about Toni's welfare. For once, her mother had not even raised the fact that the taxi fare from Gatwick Airport to Hook Norton in Oxfordshire was going to cost a fortune. She would arrange for a taxi to be waiting for her, she said, and Toni was to come straight home.

Not that she had an alternative, Toni thought bitterly as she put the telephone receiver down. She had leased her flat to a girlfriend for the next six months, and she had no wish to return to Aaron's spacious spare room, where she had spent the last week before leaving. The last thing she wanted to do was to have to face his sympathy and consolations.

Toni picked up the telephone once more and rang room service. She no longer felt nauseous but hungry, and knowing herself incapable of eating alone in the hotel restaurant, she ordered a bowl of French onion soup, a vol-au-vent filled with creamed chicken with a dish of asparagus, and some fresh fruit.

That she could contemplate eating such a large meal when she was so desperately unhappy struck her as bizarre. It could only be due to her pregnancy, she decided, and began then to worry what her parents were going to say when she told them she was going to have a baby – a child who would be fatherless. Both of them were old-fashioned, conventional, and it was the last thing they would want to face with her father still very much disabled after his stroke.

Miserably, Toni's thoughts now turned to the moment when she had actually left the yacht, Mr Metcalf holding her suitcase as he assisted her down the gangplank to the waiting taxi, Mrs Metcalf pleading with her to stay. Maurice, looking so like his twin sister, was standing at the rail beside Marisse – pretty Marisse, who had so carelessly ruined her reunion with Justin, standing at the rail, waving a chiffon scarf as if she was bidding farewell to a dear friend.

Toni's eyes filled once more with tears and she brushed them angrily away, thinking that she would never stop crying. Suddenly, unbidden, she recalled words her father had spoken when she'd told him she and Justin were going to get married.

'You haven't known him very long, sweetheart, and although I can see you are both very much in love, it doesn't necessarily mean you would be happy as man and wife. Marriage is a lifelong commitment and it is not always easy to keep your vows . . .'

She had known her father was thinking about the growing numbers of failed marriages, so often due to unfaithfulness by one partner or the other. Marriage should be for a lifetime, he'd maintained, and Toni should wait at least until the following year before tying herself for life to young Justin Metcalf, as nice a chap as he seemed to be.

Nice, yes! But not able to resist temptation even for a few months! It would seem that although he was now in his late twenties, he had still not yet grown up completely, if men ever did stop being boys at heart. He'd been flattered by the attention of that Spanish film star, Carmellia del Concordia, even though it had been only a few hours since he had made ardent love to her, Toni, the girl he was going to marry. Her father was right – she did not really know the real Justin, although despite everything that had happened, she had not stopped loving him. It was because she loved him so much that she was now feeling so terribly hurt, so betrayed.

There was a knock on the door and the room service waiter

arrived with a small trolley on which her dinner had been attrac-
tively laid. Looking at it after the waiter had departed, Toni's
eyes yet again stung with hot tears as she was reminded of the
beautiful Spanish hotel where she and Justin were to have had
their honeymoon. On one night after he had hurt his ankle, Justin
had ordered just such a meal for them, which had been brought
to their room on a similar silver trolley.

Her appetite for the food she had ordered so hungrily vanished
as she realized she would be unable to eat it. Taking only a few
mouthfuls of soup, she put down her spoon, pushed the trolley
away and lay down on one of the twin beds. Beside her, the
telephone rang. She had left instructions that she was not to be
disturbed but, the telephonist said, it was a caller speaking from
the *Silver Sprite*, who wished to speak with the utmost urgency.
Did she wish to be connected?

For a fraction of a second, Toni hesitated. She guessed it
was Justin who was ringing her. The longing to hear his voice was
almost overpowering, but she knew it was too late to repair the
damage, that words could only bring them both more unhappiness. Nothing he might say would change her mind or encourage
her to stay. She declined to take the call.

Subsequently there were three more urgent telephone messages.
The caller had asked for her room number – did she wish it to
be given? the operator enquired. The caller wished for a note
to be delivered to her room informing her that as she would not
speak to him, he would come to the hotel. The last call a quarter
of an hour later was from the hotel manager. There was a young
gentleman in the foyer demanding to see her, Toni was told.
Unfortunately the gentleman was semi-coherent and a trifle
unsteady on his feet. If perhaps mademoiselle would prefer not
to receive her visitor, he would be happy to assist him into a taxi
to take him home.

With a huge effort, Toni hardened her heart and agreed that
Justin should be sent away. Even had he been sober, there was
nothing he could have said which would eliminate what had
happened between him and Marisse. At least Marisse had been
honest enough to admit the facts which Justin had so vehemently
denied. She could still hear Marisse's voice, with its charming
French accent, saying quite matter-of-factly that 'it was just sex

between two lonely people'. And Justin's voice: 'I give you my word I have not been having an affair with Marisse!'

Burying her face in the pillow, Toni faced the fact that not only was Justin a cheat, he was also a liar.

EIGHTEEN

T he tears rolling down Marisse's face were of genuine anguish when Justin declared that he wanted nothing more to do with her, and that if she and her parents and brother did not leave the yacht the following day, he himself would do so. Furthermore he would tell them why he had asked them to go. Marisse's repeated assurances that she had sworn to Toni they had never made love had not softened Justin's attitude to her. Toni, he said bitterly, had obviously not believed her or she would not have determined to turn round and go home. He understood Toni's disbelief that the bottom half of Marisse's bikini could have found its way into his bed by mischance.

Immediately after Toni's departure, Justin had tried to find out which hotel she had gone to. He traced the taxi driver, who told Justin he had driven her to the airport hotel, and Justin made three abortive attempts to telephone her there. By the time he decided to go there in person, he had fortified himself with a steady supply of alcohol and his slurred voice, together with his unkempt appearance, endorsed the hotel manager's refusal to give him the number of Toni's room. Justin had no alternative than to allow himself to be put into a taxi and be driven back to the quayside where the *Silver Sprite* was moored.

It was Marisse's twin, Maurice, who explained to his parents and their host and hostess why Toni had suddenly departed. Although Maurice made no mention of the bikini, he told them that his twin's flirtatious manner with Justin had been mistaken by Toni for a more serious relationship, as a result of which she had opted to go home.

Justin's return from the airport almost too drunk to stand up, combined with Marisse's refusal to leave her cabin, were enough to convince Monsieur and Madame Bourget that their flirtatious daughter was the cause of this cataclysm, and they said that regretfully they would disembark the following morning. When

Maurice informed his twin that they were all leaving, for once the tears Marisse shed were genuine. What had started when she first met Justin as an amusing flirtation quickly became a frustrated physical passion, the sparks inflamed by Justin's refusal to succumb to her overt demands.

It was the first time in Marisse's young life that a member of the opposite sex had failed to respond to her flirtation. So strong were her feelings for Justin that she concluded that she had fallen in love with him. Determined to come between him and the English fiancée who stood in her way, she'd devised her plan.

The plan had succeeded in so far as Toni was on her way home, but now it was about to be dashed. Tomorrow morning, she and Maurice and her parents would be leaving the yacht, and she did not know if she would ever see Justin again.

Her face was pale, her eyes ringed with sleeplessness and tears as she stood the next morning between her parents as they said their goodbyes to their hosts. There was no sign of Justin, and Marisse went to stand beside Maurice. She guessed that Justin would be feeling anything but sympathetic towards her because this enjoyable part of their family holiday had come to a premature end.

When the taxi drove the Bourget family down the quayside away from the yacht, Maurice found himself wondering whether Justin and Marisse had indeed been having an affair. Close as he was to his twin, it was not something he intended to ask her. He hoped not, although he suspected the worst. As the taxi turned a corner and the *Silver Sprite* disappeared from sight, he found himself more concerned about the unhappy English girl than he was for his tearful twin clinging to his side.

The sight of Aaron's tall figure coming towards her at Gatwick Airport unexpectedly reduced Toni to tears. Throughout the flight home, she had remained dry-eyed as she tried to keep thoughts of her parting with Justin from her mind. She'd told herself that what had transpired was, in the long term, a good thing, revealing his wayward nature and preventing her from marrying the wrong person.

Before leaving the yacht the previous afternoon, she had been on the point of giving Justin the benefit of the doubt about his relationship with Marisse. Nothing could have been less anticipated than Marisse's sudden appearance and her confession of their affair. Unfaithfulness was clearly not deemed of particular importance to the French girl – or, supposedly to Justin. He'd strenuously denied an ongoing affair, but Marisse had told a different story, proving it was impossible for Justin to stay faithful to her even for three or four months.

Now, here was Aaron, her good friend, offering her a large, clean handkerchief, wheeling her suitcase with one hand and tucking his other arm through hers, walking her out of the building towards the car park. To her relief, his casual enquiries about her flight did not include questions about the reason why she had returned home so unexpectedly or what had transpired to cause her tears.

Tired and emotionally exhausted as she was, it had been a huge relief to see Aaron's familiar tall figure waiting for her, and now, when they reached his car, it was a further relief when he announced that instead of putting her on a train, he was intending to drive her home to her parents in his new, luxurious Jaguar. All she could think of now was the safe familiarity of her own teenage bedroom awaiting her at home and her mother telling her that it was 'all for the best', her answer to all Toni's girlish distress when she quarrelled with her school friends. Not without bitterness, she reflected that both her parents had warned her against marrying Justin before she had known him a lot longer.

During the journey down to Hook Norton, Aaron did all the talking. He'd left untouched the spare room in his flat which she had used, he told her; and if she wanted to come back to London – renew her job, perhaps – she would be welcome to make use of the room for as long as she wished. He spoke briefly of the articles about Japan he had written which were to be published by the *National Geographic* magazine, and which he was eager to show her.

They were nearing Banbury before Toni could bring herself to speak. 'I really do appreciate your meeting me, Aaron,' she said. 'It was quite remiss of my mother to have bothered you: I could have come by train.'

'Toni, your mother was quite right to ring and tell me you were coming home. She thought you sounded unwell, and she remembered me telling her when I last saw her that if ever there was anything I could do for you in return for all your kindness to me, she must promise to let me know.'

The words brought fresh tears to Toni's eyes. She said huskily, 'Aaron, I'm really so glad you were there.' She paused briefly and, not wanting him to suspect the real reason for her return home, added: 'I didn't want to worry my mother, but the truth is I had been feeling unwell and I really wasn't fit to go travelling.'

She broke off, thinking how absurd her words sounded: flying to the south of France by aeroplane was hardly an exacting journey! Moreover, if she was unwell, there was no better way to recuperate than on a leisurely holiday on a yacht in the Mediterranean. She was unsure whether Aaron believed her or not, as the only comment he made was that she should see her doctor as soon as possible as she wasn't looking well.

'I expect you need a tonic!' he remarked as he turned down the lane leading to Hook Norton.

Toni managed a weak smile. 'You sounded just like my father, Aaron. He always recommended "a good tonic" for whatever I was suffering from as a child, be it measles, chickenpox, tooth-ache or even a bad cold!'

Pleased to see her smile, Aaron said, '"A week with daily walks along the promenade for some bracing sea air!" That's what the matron at my prep school used to say whenever one of us small boys was in the school san. Maybe I should take you down to Brighton or Bournemouth or some other seaside resort and get some colour into your cheeks.'

Toni managed another smile. 'Stop being kind to me, Aaron!' she said. 'You're making me feel sorry for myself!'

It was on the tip of Aaron's tongue to ask her what was the real reason for her to feel sorry for herself, but he sensed this was not the moment. All that mattered was that Toni's reunion with her boyfriend had turned out to be a disaster. Now she was back in England, here at his side, he was not going to let her leave him again if he could possibly prevent it.

*   *   *

When they arrived, Mrs Ward did not ply her daughter with questions for once as Aaron took Toni's suitcase out of the car and followed them into the house. He returned to retrieve Toni's jacket and, collecting the presents he had brought from the back seat, he followed them indoors.

'Let's all have a nice cup of tea,' Mrs Ward said as she led them into the kitchen. 'We'll open our presents in a minute. How very kind of you, Mr Osborn.'

What a nice man he is, she thought. She had nothing against Justin, who had seemed to be a very nice young man, but as she had said to her husband, Justin had not seemed mature or responsible enough to look after their little girl. Toni, they had agreed, should be marrying someone older, more reliable, like the nice Mr Osborn who was proving to be such a good friend to her – and indeed to them, too. He'd never arrived without some thoughtful gift and always took time to talk to them. They also admired the brave way he hid his grief over his wife's untimely death. He had only once spoken of it himself, when in a shaky voice he had referred to a tragedy so unbearable that he'd wished he, too, had died. Then he had quickly changed the subject and spoken of the wonderful care he'd received at Stoke Mandeville Hospital.

Aaron tactfully stayed only long enough to have a cup of tea and say hello to Mr Ward before returning to London. He would come down again in a day or two, he said, when hopefully Toni would be feeling better and he could take her out for lunch.

Far from feeling better, Toni felt worse with each day that passed. She had pains in her abdomen, was feeling sick again from time to time, but despite her mother's frequent requests for her to see the doctor, Toni delayed doing so, insisting there was nothing wrong with her. She had hoped Justin would be pleased when she told him she would be having his baby, but had no doubt as to how shocked her parents would be if she were to announce she was to have a fatherless child. She was far from sure how she would cope without their support. One thing was for certain: she would not allow Justin to become involved.

It was now nearly four months since she and Justin had made passionate love the night before he'd left to join his family abroad. Her thickening waist and fuller breasts left her in no further doubt as to her condition. When finally she did see their family doctor, he confirmed her pregnancy, and she confessed her fears about breaking the news to her parents. As she did not intend to marry the father of the baby, she told him, it was not going to make them happy.

'I shall go back to London and consider what I am going to do,' she told him. 'As I am no longer going to marry the baby's father, I wish I wasn't having it.'

The doctor regarded her anxiously. 'I should advise you, my dear, that you do not have much time to consider a termination,' he said. 'If you are concerned about your finances, there are a number of different allowances and assistance provided by the government.' He'd known her since she was a little girl and was personally concerned for her. 'Is there no chance you and the father might be reconciled?' he asked gently. 'Perhaps when he hears he is to be a father . . .'

'No!' Toni broke in swiftly. 'I'm not going to tell him.' She broke off as a picture of the French girl's orange bikini in Justin's bed came into her mind. She could hear Marisse's voice saying: '*It was just sex between two lonely people . . .*' Perhaps, she told herself, there were girls who would overlook that kind of betrayal, think nothing of it: it was just sex, not love. Maybe she was being old-fashioned thinking that physical faithfulness mattered to partners, married or otherwise. But remembering the close, passionate intimacy she and Justin had shared, the thought of him having sex with another girl was intolerable. Nor could she overlook the fact that he had denied it – lied to her. She had believed him and then Marisse had admitted the facts.

The doctor now interrupted her thoughts, saying: 'You must register with another medical practice in London, Antonia, if you intend staying there for any length of time. If you return home, I shall be very happy to see you through this. You mustn't let it get you down, my dear,' he added with a gentle smile. 'As you know, single mothers are quite the norm these days!'

Toni returned his smile, thanked him and left the surgery. If nothing else, she told herself as she drove home, the visit had helped her to make up her mind. For the time being, she would definitely not tell her parents about the baby. She would accept Aaron's offer and go back to London and stay in his spare room whilst she waited for the tenant renting her old flat to find somewhere else to go. She would find a temporary job to support herself for as long as she could, and not touch her meagre savings. Somehow she would manage and, meanwhile, she was fortunate to have Aaron for a friend. One thing she would not do, she promised herself, was take advantage of his kindness. It was true that she had proved to be a good friend to him when he needed it and she could understand his wish to be there for her.

It would be very different if she could have relied upon her parents' support, Toni reflected as she drove down the narrow road to Hook Norton village, but she knew only too well how horrified they would be – how vehemently they would try to persuade her to heal the rift with Justin and marry him as quickly as possible in order to legitimize the baby. The shock might even set back her father's recovery. She would have to tell them eventually but not until she had everything under control – a job, her own flat, her plans for an independent future – so that they need not acknowledge the baby if they were ashamed to do so.

As she drove home Toni allowed herself to think how different her present situation would have been had Justin not proved to be such a perfidious cheat. Had Marisse not been so careless as to leave her clothing in his bed, she would never have known that he had been unfaithful to her. Much as she wanted to do so, she could not bring herself to believe he would have confessed had there been no evidence to the contrary. Had he done so she might have been able to forgive him. It was not just his succumbing to a momentary sexual invitation but the fact that he had denied it and lied to her, making it impossible for her ever to trust him again.

Reaching home, she found her mother sitting at the kitchen table waiting anxiously to be reassured that there was nothing seriously wrong with her precious daughter. She accepted Toni's muttered 'A bit run down!' without question and, smiling, told her that the nice Aaron Osborn had been on the telephone to enquire after her health.

'Such a caring man!' Mrs Ward said as she pulled out a chair for Toni and started to cook their lunch. 'You know, darling, a man like that must have been a wonderful husband.' She paused a moment to inspect a casserole she was about to put in the oven, before adding, 'He reminds me a little of your dear father – he was always so thoughtful, so attentive. It was why I fell in love with him. Perhaps you . . .'

'No, Mum!' Toni broke in sharply. 'Aaron and I are just very good friends, and I haven't the slightest wish to marry anyone, thank you very much.'

'Of course, my darling!' Mrs Ward said quickly, reproaching herself for not appreciating that her daughter was probably more hurt than angry about Justin's interest in the French girl. She had not been particularly surprised when Toni had finally told her what happened. Justin was far too young to be married. Mr Osborn, by contrast, was a charming, mature man who she deemed eminently trustworthy.

As she laid the table, Mrs Ward reflected happily that their nice doctor had told Toni there was nothing to worry about. Her daughter was now safely home with a clean bill of health, and although Toni was presently unhappy about the break-up of her relationship with Justin, despite her protests the future looked promising.

'You must ring Mr Osborn and tell him he will be most welcome to come for Sunday lunch,' she said. 'We could have a joint of beef; it hasn't seemed economical buying a joint just for your father and me. I can make one of my Yorkshire puddings and . . .'

Toni stopped listening. Personally, she did not care whether Aaron came to lunch or not. She was glad to see her mother happy and tried not to feel guilty, knowing that one word from her about the baby would without doubt wipe every trace of happiness from her mother's face.

NINETEEN

Nadine Metcalf regarded her son's unmistakably hungover face with a mixture of affection and exasperation. Having gone in search of Toni the previous evening, Justin had not returned until daylight that morning. Still befuddled enough to trip on the gangway before barging into his parents' cabin instead of his own, his apologies had been indecipherable. It was late afternoon before she saw him again, pale-faced but coherent. He was stretched out on one of the sun loungers under the shade of the striped awning. She seated herself on the edge of the adjoining lounger.

'So! I take it my naughty boy failed to persuade his *inamorata* to return!' She pushed her Versace sunglasses up to her fashionably coiffed, highlighted hair and gave a gentle tap with a scarlet-tipped finger to the side of her son's pale cheek. Her tone of voice suddenly became more serious. 'Really, Justin, I would have thought a child of mine – and indeed, your father's – would have behaved with a little more common sense, let alone discretion. If you did indeed have *un petit frisson* with Mademoiselle Marisse, how could you possibly be so careless as to leave evidence of the fact in your bed when you knew Toni was due to arrive at any moment!'

'Mama!' Justin interrupted, rubbing his tired, sore eyes with the back of his hand. 'I don't know who gave you the facts but I *did not* have sex with Marisse. Not once! Is that clear? Yes, there were occasions when I could have succumbed to her requests, but I didn't!'

His mother's eyebrows rose sceptically. 'Darling boy, you do not have to play the innocent with me. I saw how that pretty young mademoiselle was doing her utmost to make herself attractive to you. She—'

'Mother!' Justin interrupted a second time, his voice now sharper. '*I did not fuck Marisse!* Why can't you and Toni believe me? I did not—'

It was his mother's turn to interrupt. 'I may be what you kindly call a "with-it" parent, Justin, but I don't care for that sort of language. Keep it for your friends, if you must. But that is not why I have come to talk to you. When young Toni left yesterday afternoon I was not surprised to hear that you had gone after her. The next thing I heard was your noisy, unmistakeably drunken return to the *Sprite* this morning. Incoherent as you were when you barged into my cabin instead of your own, I gathered that you had not been successful in persuading Toni to come back. So how come you are lying here as if nothing was wrong? Aren't you going back to England to convince the poor girl of your innocence – that is, if you are indeed as innocent as you say?'

Seeing the mutinous expression on her son's face, she added quickly, 'I'm not questioning your innocence, my darling, only the way you are – or should I say are *not* – dealing with the matter. At least Marisse is off your hands. Your father, needless to say, is very put out. He was enjoying his games of chess with Monsieur Bourget. However, that is not my concern. What I want to know, Justin, is this: when you have recovered from your hangover, are you going to England? I am hoping very much that this is not the end of your relationship with Toni. I've always been very fond of her, and both your father and I thought she would be the perfect wife for you.'

Justin's pale face reflected his opposing reactions. His expression was a mixture of defiance and misery as he said, 'I thought I had convinced Toni that I'd not been unfaithful to her. She actually told me so, and then . . .' His voice deepened with distress. 'Then she suddenly changed her mind, although Marisse says she swears on the bible that she told Toni we hadn't been having an affair. Even if she didn't believe Marisse, if she really loved me she could at the very least have given me the benefit of the doubt. But no! Just because Marisse happens to be pretty, and you know that flirtatious way she has, and calling me *cheri* all the time . . . Toni just put two and two together and made five. If she really loved me,' he repeated, 'the very least she could have done was give me the benefit of the doubt when I told her I hadn't the slightest idea how that stupid bit of Marisse's bikini got into my bed. Frankly, if Toni thinks that I'd lie to her about it, what sort of relationship do we have? She upset everyone dashing off in a temper and she wouldn't even talk to me, let alone see me last night at the hotel when I tried to have another go at making her see sense. The stupid receptionist refused to give me her room number without her permission, presumably because by then I'd had a few drinks . . . So what was I supposed to do?'

Justin's mother looked at her son's unhappy face and sighed. 'Quite right, too. Like most men, you can be extraordinarily stupid when you've overstepped the mark. I'm not surprised Toni refused to see you.' She gave a deep sigh. 'My darling boy, the facts now are these: Toni has left you and I am asking you a very simple question – do you still love her? If she really is the girl you want to marry, I strongly recommend that you don't just lie here nursing your resentment at her reactions. Frankly I think I, too, would have behaved just as she did in my younger days if I had been reunited with your father only to find a girl's underwear in his bed!'

Justin scowled. 'Are you suggesting I go chasing after Toni again when she has made it perfectly clear that she doesn't want anything more to do with me? Anyway, I'm not the one who's guilty!' he protested. 'Why should I go and say I'm sorry? I'm damn well not sorry. I almost wish I had . . . well, that I *had* had an affair with Marisse and had something to be sorry for!'

Nadine Metcalf managed to conceal a smile. Justin sounded exactly as he'd done at six years old when his nanny had punished him for breaking a vase he'd not touched. 'I repeat my question, darling,' she said gently. 'Do you still love Toni?'

For a brief moment, colour flared in Justin's pale cheeks. 'Well, of course I do! But—'

'No, no buts!' his mother interrupted. 'I will book you on a flight home in a few days, after you have had time to sober up and think this through. You know, Justin, I'll bet you anything you like that at this moment, your beloved is every bit as unhappy as you are and wishing she had not departed so hastily.'

Toni unlocked the suitcase Aaron had lifted on to the bed in the spare room of his flat and began to put away her clothes in the drawers and wardrobe. With a stab of misery, she reflected that it was only a few days since she had packed this same suitcase in the same room in Aaron's flat in preparation for her flight to France and her reunion with Justin. She had been full of wonderful expectations and then their reunion had turned out to be the very opposite of her dreams.

Tears stung her eyes as she withdrew from the tissue paper the sexy Lise Charmel ivory lace nightie she had bought for Justin's benefit. Unworn, still expertly folded by the shop that had sold it to her, it was just one of the variety of small surprises she had bought to please him – a bottle of his favourite aftershave, a small tin of the Eccles cakes he loved. She had also planned to surprise him with a pair of Ray-Ban sunglasses for him to use as replacements when, as he so often did, he mislaid his own identical ones. They had remained unpacked in her suitcase which, when it was emptied, she put on top of the spacious wardrobe in the corner of the room.

She was now filled with a huge sense of relief when she finally sat down on the edge of the bed. For the first time in her life, she had been glad to say goodbye to her parents when Aaron arrived at Cherry Tree Cottage to drive her back to London. Her mother had been fussing continuously about her health, and she'd feared that at any moment she would guess she was pregnant. That was the last thing she wished to reveal, knowing how distressed her mother would feel, especially when she had still not fully recovered from the shock of her husband's stroke.

Somewhat to Toni's surprise, her mother seemed to have complete faith in Aaron's assurances that he could be trusted to look after her.

Aaron had been his usual caring self as he drove away from the cottage and headed for the M40 motorway. Sensing Toni's mood, he'd done all the talking. When eventually they reached his flat, she found he had put a beautiful vase of roses on her dressing table and a parcel containing a Mulberry tote handbag with a note saying: *Welcome! Treat this as your home for as long as you wish, Toni.*

She was both touched and hugely embarrassed by his present, wishing he had not been so extravagant. His caring attentions, if such they could be called, were so painfully in contrast with Justin's behaviour. Now that she'd had time to calm down, it crossed her mind that she might – just *might* – have misjudged him; that after all he *could* have been telling the truth when he'd proclaimed he'd never had a relationship with Marisse. Then she recalled the sight of Marisse standing beside the bed where she herself and Justin had not long made love, admitting in her attractive French accent that she and Justin were just two lonely people who had shared sex but not love. Marisse seemed to think that Justin's unfaithfulness was something she should overlook.

For the hundredth time since she'd left the yacht, Toni's mind mulled over the events surrounding her arrival in France and hasty departure. Was it possible, she asked herself now, wanting so much for it to be true, that Marisse had planted her bikini in Justin's bed in the hope that she would behave exactly as she had and go back to England? If Marisse had truly fallen in love with Justin, she might well have chosen that very way to end her relationship with Justin, leaving the field clear for herself.

Here now in Aaron's spare room, Toni's heart hardened as she recalled Justin's lie that he'd not had sex with Marisse. She would never be able to trust him again. It was all over between them and there was no way she could marry him now, believing as she did that there had to be trust in a relationship.

Unfortunately, she realized, despite everything, even though she could never forgive Justin, she still loved him, and now . . . Well, now that she was carrying his child, she needed him more than ever. So strong was the feeling that she even found herself querying whether a few sexual transgressions really did matter so much.

TWENTY

B e it fate, coincidence, karma or destiny, Toni's reflections when she was unpacking her suitcase were to have a momentous effect upon her life. While she was hanging her clothes in the wardrobe, the telephone rang in Aaron's lavish sitting room. Aaron put down the newspaper, in which he had been studying the previous day's movements of his shares, and picked up the receiver. There was a moment's silence before the caller enquired: 'Can I speak to Toni Ward, please?'

Aaron paused as he tried to identify the male voice, then enquired who was calling. 'Justin, Justin Metcalf. I couldn't get Toni on her mobile and her mother told me Toni had left it by mistake when she went to London this morning, with you. She gave me your number. I wish to speak to Toni, please.'

'Well, yes, Toni is staying here. But I'm afraid she isn't here right now. She told me one of her friends invited her to a movie – something she was keen to see – and on to a party afterwards. I'm going out later myself but I will leave her a note saying you called. Do you have a number I can give her?'

With an effort, Justin hid his disappointment. Trying not to feel resentful that Osborn was apparently masterminding Toni's life, he explained that she did have his mobile number and she was to ring him that evening whatever time she returned.

'Of course!' Aaron replied smoothly. 'She might be late, since she's going to this party, but I've promised to pick her up in my car if she can't get a lift back.'

Justin put down his phone and sat for a moment in one of the white leather armchairs in his parents' luxurious London apartment. He had expected to return to his flat, which he had left in the hands of the caretaker for the duration of his absence abroad. Unaware of his decision to return to England or where to contact him, the agents had authorized builders to go in and repair the extensive damage caused by faulty plumbing in the flat above. On his arrival from France that afternoon, Justin had turned his back on the mess and gone round to his parents' apartment in Grosvenor House.

His sudden arrival there was unexpected by the domestic staff who had not removed the dust sheets from the furniture. The empty room compounded his depression at not being able to talk to Toni.

His hangover a thing of the past, he had boarded his flight to England in a mood of optimism. His mother had made him see things from Toni's point of view; that her reaction, if a little extreme, was justified. When he had calmed down he'd admitted to himself that whilst it was true he had not been unfaithful with Marisse, there had been quite a few times when he'd come very close to it. She'd made it abundantly clear that she wanted him, flaunting her not inconsiderable sexual attributes on every possible occasion. He'd told his mother Toni should have been congratulating him on his restraint rather than condemning him. Not that he was going to say so to Toni. His mother had pointed out that it was up to him to restore Toni's faith in his innocence if he wished to renew their relationship.

His heart had lifted at the thought and it had been quite a shock to hear from Toni's parents when he'd phoned them from the airport that far from being with them as he had supposed, she had gone to London and was staying with the guy who'd had the skiing accident in Spain – Osborn, Aaron Osborn. Although he'd felt sorry for the guy when he'd met him briefly one time at Stoke Mandeville, he hadn't taken to him. Granted, Osborn had been decent enough letting Toni use his London flat whilst she was waiting to fly out and join him on the yacht. She'd been able to lease her own flat to a girl friend who had wanted to move in immediately, and Toni had told him that Osborn had refused to accept any contribution towards her expenses. At the time, he had disliked the thought that Toni was indebted to the guy. The same uneasiness had returned when Mrs Ward had told him Toni was once again staying in Osborn's flat.

He was jealous, Justin realized as he went to the drinks cupboard in the deserted dining room to get himself a whisky, and he had no right to be. Toni had assured him that her relationship with Aaron Osborn was completely platonic. Possibly it was platonic on her side, Justin told himself now as he tried absent-mindedly to call up the news on the huge TV screen on the wall, but he doubted very much that Osborn was immune to Toni's charms. When he himself had seen her looking so pretty, so desirable, as she'd walked towards him out of Customs at Nice Airport, he'd felt an overwhelming wave of love for her and a fierce desire to make love to her there and then.

Sinking back into one of the large armchairs, he allowed his thoughts to return to the scene in his cabin on board the *Silver Sprite*. How *had* that stupid bit of Marisse's bikini got into his bed? Once or twice she had entered his cabin after a swim wearing it under a towelling robe, but on both occasions he had told her to go and get dressed as she was dripping water over his floor. He would hardly have failed to notice if she'd left his cabin half naked. Justin caught his breath as he recalled how he had found her semi-naked body so annoyingly attractive, and had it not been for his determination to stay faithful to the girl he loved, he might well have given in to temptation with Marisse. It was bitterly frustrating, therefore, that Toni should have assumed him guilty and rushed off in that cavalier way.

He looked at his wristwatch and saw that it was still only nine o'clock, or twenty-one hours as his father, a former army officer, would insist upon saying. It was far too early for Toni to have returned to Osborn's flat and found his message. Restless and anxious, he badly wanted another drink, but recalling the catastrophic result of his last heavy drinking session, he decided to remain sober. As his mother had pointed out to him, had he not turned up in such a state at Toni's hotel, he might have been able to see her and persuade her not to go rushing back to England.

For the third time since he'd let himself into his parents' suite, Justin tried to turn his attention to the television. There were highlights of a football match showing, which would normally have engaged his attention, but his thoughts returned once more to Toni. He'd been right in assuming that she would go home to her parents when she flew back to England, but he was surprised when Mrs Ward told him Toni had gone back to London in a hurry and left her mobile behind.

Justin tried to quell the stab of suspicion he'd felt on hearing Toni was back in Osborn's flat. Was it possible, he asked himself, that the guy was more than just a kind friend who happened to have a spare room in his flat? Might he and Toni have become more than just friends? Had Toni fallen for the guy and jumped at the excuse Marisse's bikini had given her to call it a day with him?

Somehow Justin couldn't believe Toni capable of such devious behaviour. In her many text messages before she had left to join him in France, she had sounded as loving and excited at the thought of their forthcoming reunion as he was, and her few references to Aaron Osborn were no more than off-hand remarks about his hospitality and kind-heartedness – that it was his way of repayment for her visits to him when he was recovering from the accident which had so nearly killed him.

Justin could understand Osborn's wish to level the playing field, but it was questionable whether the guy was immune to Toni's undoubted sex appeal. On the other hand the man's wife had met a horrible death, and it seemed highly unlikely that her husband, who'd nearly lost his own life trying to save her, would be looking for a replacement so soon after the tragedy.

Justin glanced at his watch once more – not quite ten o'clock. His mobile was silent. For the eighth time, he checked that it was properly switched on. He waited another hour and then rang Aaron Osborn again, only to be told that Toni had not yet returned, and that he was going to bed but would leave another message on Toni's pillow where she could not fail to see it. He also reassured Justin that he had followed his instructions and emphasized that she should ring Justin no matter how late it was.

As the minutes, the quarter hours, and finally the hours ticked by, Justin's hopes of a reconciliation with Toni that night dwindled. He recalled his mother's words of wisdom. *'Just tell the girl you love her!'* she had said. *'Right now she's probably regretting that she flew off home in such a hurry.'* On the contrary, he thought bitterly, Toni was out having a fun evening somewhere, not sitting by herself as he was, filled with regrets, wishing they could be together. He could only hope that when she did eventually return to Osborn's flat, she would ring him. He'd said it didn't matter how late she was back.

It was two o'clock in the morning when Justin finally gave up hope of hearing Toni's voice. His bitter disappointment could not be assuaged by the vain thought that either her silence was because Osborn had not given her his messages or that she had failed to find them. What he now feared was that she had read them and decided to ignore them.

Tiredness, disappointment and bitterness now merged with anger as Justin reflected that Toni clearly did not love him as much as he had loved her. She hadn't felt it was important enough to establish the facts before condemning him, and now, when he had set his injured feelings to one side and followed her back to England to put things right between them, she had chosen to risk ditching their relationship forever. Well, he did not intend to crawl back asking for her forgiveness when he was perfectly innocent. Even though she might be justified in still having doubts about Marisse's stupid bikini, it would have cost her no more than a phone call to hear him trying once more to establish the truth – that he knew nothing about its presence in his bed.

So much for her undying love for him, he thought bitterly. He could have understood her initial reaction, believing him guilty, but not this apparent refusal to speak to him. His mother had been wrong in believing he could put things right by following Toni back to England.

His mind made up, Justin went to the cabinet and poured himself another whisky – a double this time – before walking wearily into the spare bedroom. The heating had not yet been turned on and he realized he was still wearing his light-weight south of France clothes. Shivering as he removed them, he climbed into bed and turned off the light. It was so unfair, he told himself miserably: he had done nothing wrong! On the contrary, he had spent weeks eschewing Marisse's flirtatious invitations, determined to be faithful to Toni.

Unless Toni phoned him before ten o'clock next morning, he told himself, he was taking the train to Gatwick Airport where he would catch the next flight to Nice.

Only a few miles away, Toni was turning restlessly in her bed. Sleepless, she tried to fight the memory of Marisse's confession. When this was not going in circles round her head, her thoughts turned to the baby she was carrying: whether it would be a boy or a girl; whether Justin would have been upset or thrilled to hear of its existence; whether they would have got married at once or waited until after the baby was born. It even went through her mind to question whether his sexual faithlessness really was so important to her, especially as the French girl herself had implied that her affair with Justin had been merely physical, not love.

'Oh, Justin!' she wept into her pillow. 'I need you so much! I'd give the world to be able to pick up my phone and talk to you – tell you I still love you, and hear your voice saying you still love me.'

She lifted her hand to turn off the bedside light, and saw the glass of water beside it. There, too, was her bedside clock, a box of tissues and the watch she had removed from her wrist. It was as well she didn't have her mobile or she might have been tempted to call Justin just to hear his voice, she thought miserably. But there was no mobile phone, nor was there a note saying Justin had phoned requesting her to ring him regardless of the hour, and that he was waiting anxiously for her call.

TWENTY-ONE

Aaron was once again standing at his sitting-room window staring at the dark skeletons of the leafless trees on the common. It was a habit that had formed ever since he had leased this flat when he'd come out of hospital and discovered the therapeutic effect of the scene. High above the streets below, the view was devoid of human beings and he could work out solutions to his problems without distractions.

He turned now to look at Toni who was at the opposite end of the room, curled up in one of the big armchairs, her legs tucked under her, talking on her mobile to her former boss.

Aaron's jaw tightened as he listened to Toni's voice filled with enthusiasm about a job which might be available. By then, she was saying, she would have found a flat; the old one she'd shared with a friend was still occupied by her replacement. It was at that point he realized he was going to lose her. Until then, he had not allowed himself to think that her return to him from France might not be permanent. Since her confession that she was pregnant, he had convinced himself that she would continue to allow him to take care of her, that she now needed him to deputize for Metcalf as a provider for her and her child. So far, he had managed to keep Metcalf at bay, and the man had been gullible enough on each occasion he'd left messages for Toni to assume that Aaron had passed them on.

'There's absolutely no hurry for you to move out, Toni. You know you are more than welcome to stay here,' he said when she'd finished her phone conversation. 'I wish you would bin those brochures, too!' he continued, pointing to the bunch of papers she was perusing. 'You've been trudging round looking for a flat you can afford for weeks!'

Toni caught her breath as she glanced briefly at Aaron's face. His expression was usually caring, solicitous and encouraging, but of late it had been almost impatient. She knew why, and was not surprised when, as expected, he had raised the subject of her moving out yet again.

'It's really quite unnecessary,' he was insisting. 'Here is this large flat of which I only occupy a third. As I said the other day, Toni, you can pay me a nominal rent if that's what is bothering you.' His voice suddenly deepened and it seemed to Toni that his grey eyes darkened. 'Or have I missed the point and you are wanting your own place in case the errant boyfriend reappears on the scene?'

Toni's cheeks turned a deep pink, her discomfiture arising partly from Aaron's description of Justin, but also from the fact that he was acting like her carer – a possessive carer – and she was finding his devotion embarrassing. Now well into the fifth month of her pregnancy, she had started to feel the baby move. Each time that happened, her thoughts turned to Justin, and she badly wanted to be able to say to him, 'Feel it, Justin! Our baby!' Had the break-up of their relationship been brought about by her, she would long since have pleaded for his forgiveness, but it had been Justin's affair with Marisse that was to blame.

The irony of the situation was that Aaron was behaving exactly as she would have wanted Justin to behave. Not that there was any physical intimacy in her relationship with Aaron. She would not have wanted him to feel the baby move, or do more than kiss her cheek, but what she did so appreciate was the exceptional care he took of her in every other way.

From time to time the thought had crossed her mind that Aaron wanted more from her than a platonic friendship. Even her mother had questioned the relationship, pointing out that there would be something wrong with any young man who did not want 'greater intimacies', as she had phrased it, living with the woman they loved. She insisted that Aaron was very much in love with her and hinted that he would make an excellent husband.

Mrs Ward was now finally aware that her daughter was soon to give birth to an illegitimate baby, and when she had got over the initial shock, was praying that Toni would do the right and sensible thing and marry Aaron – a man who seemed to her to epitomize everything a girl might want in a husband. He was handsome, rich, a widower and he obviously adored Toni. He was even prepared to overlook the fact that her daughter was pregnant with another man's child. That, surely, was love! She took hope from the fact that Toni was still living in Aaron's flat as if she were his wife, she said to her husband, and as far as Toni was concerned, she might protest their relationship was purely platonic, but she herself considered it was 'only a matter of time'.

Not far from tears, Toni was silently acknowledging that her desperate desire to move into her own flat was in part motivated by the fact that she could no longer doubt that Aaron was in love with her. She had been so wrapped up in her own unhappiness that she'd given no serious thought to his feelings. It was now imperative that she moved to her own place.

Picking up and reading one of the brochures, Aaron stared down at her with a strange expression which she found disconcerting.

'Consider this!' he said in a strangely harsh tone. *'One-room flat, fourth floor, near Victoria station.'* Have you thought what climbing those stairs would be like in your condition? Exhausting, to say the least, if not dangerous! As for the job you told me your old boss might offer you . . .'

'I have already told Julia I can't work full time once the baby is born!' Toni interrupted unhappily. Julia had been dismayed when Toni had told her about the baby during lunch one day after Toni's return to London. Deeply concerned for her, Julia had then offered to find her part-time work she could do at home on her computer. She knew Toni's parents were managing to survive on their pensions but would not be able to add to her income. Also aware of this, Aaron had quickly pointed out that she should remain here in his flat where she would have no rent to pay. Her mother, Toni thought wearily, would probably want her to stay with Aaron at least until after the baby was born.

'I think we should get married!'

Aaron's words, spoken in a firm, level tone, drained the colour from Toni's cheeks. He had spoken so casually that he might have been suggesting they went out for a walk or a meal.

Seeing the stunned expression on Toni's face, Aaron said quickly: 'Don't look so shocked!' He forced a smile as he added: 'I'm fully aware that you had intended marrying Metcalf, that you were in love with him before you discovered he wasn't to be trusted. But that is in the past, Toni, and as Fate would have it, I've fallen in love with you. I want to be the one to take care of you, and furthermore, I'll give the child you're carrying a name – my name!'

Toni's face was shocked as he continued quickly: 'I know you look on me only as a friend, and for the time being, I'm not asking anything more than that. You see, I truly believe you will feel quite differently after the child is born, and we become a family.'

He broke off, his eyes staring into hers in such a way as to give her a sudden frisson of fear. It was not what Aaron had said which she found so disturbing, but the way he was looking at her – a way she could not have described but which was almost threatening. She felt mortified as the realization hit her that she must somehow have given Aaron reason to think that she would ever consider such a thing. His proposal had almost sounded like a threat: *'Marry me or else.'*

She caught her breath and tried to keep her voice steady as she replied: 'I'm so very sorry if I have misled you, Aaron. I mean, I believed we were friends – just ordinary friends. You knew how I felt about Justin, and I knew you must still be grieving for your wife, and . . .'

'And none of that stopped me falling in love with you, Toni,' he broke in harshly. His tone softening, he continued: 'I believe we could be happy together – we are happy together.' Momentarily, his voice hardened as he said, 'Your boyfriend . . . he isn't coming back to heal the rift, is he? He doesn't love you enough to eat humble pie. For God's sake, Toni, I'd have come looking for you weeks ago rather than risk losing you. Let me take care of you! If we were married quickly, I could legitimize your baby and relieve your parents of any distress. I love you, Toni, very, very much.'

Toni caught her breath. She was on the point of arguing that it was she who had left Justin, not the other way round, but Aaron had sounded so sincere, so caring, that the last thing she wanted was to argue with him. She must now make it absolutely clear to him that, despite everything that had happened, she was still in love with Justin. Nor must she give Aaron any false hopes that she might marry him: not to legitimize her baby, nor to please her parents, nor because as a single mother she needed his support.

Toni's mind was racing as she considered Aaron's unexpected proposal. He was certainly right in believing her hopes that Justin would seek to make amends were unfounded. Quite probably, he was even now enjoying the attributes of the pretty French girl, and she, Toni, was the last thing on his mind. She no longer had any hope that he would suddenly reappear in her life and beg her forgiveness. Too much time had passed without any attempt on his part to do so.

The loss of hope for a reconciliation, she thought now, in no way affected her reactions to Aaron's unexpected proposal. She could not possibly consider marrying him, good friend though he was. Life might be difficult to manage at the moment but at least she had Justin's baby to give it purpose. It was an immensely kind gesture of Aaron's to give the baby his name in order to legitimize it and, indeed, to care for her and the baby in the future, but she wanted her child to grow up knowing who his real father was – perhaps even meeting him one day.

'I'm really, really sorry, Aaron,' she said quietly. 'I so much appreciate everything you have done for me and for being such a wonderful friend. You are my very best friend, and I wish it could have been something more, but . . .' Anxious to lessen his disappointment, she added: 'But it wouldn't work, Aaron. For a start, I could never stop thinking of Justin, not now when I'm having his baby. When it's born, if it looks like him . . .'

She broke off, too full of emotion to continue. For a moment Aaron, too, was speechless. There was a strange expression on his face which Toni found vaguely unnerving. Although she knew it could not possibly be so, it seemed as if he was not so much disappointed by her rejection as angry. Then, quite suddenly, he smiled.

'I must apologize for being so insensitive,' he said. 'I daresay if it were us, the men, who got pregnant, we'd understand women's feelings a great deal better than we do. Please forgive me, Toni. I think I was motivated to propose we got married by the fact that you were having such a bad time of it – homeless and without the love and support you should be getting.' His smile was now gentle and familiar as he added: 'Not that I want you to forget the offer, which still stands, and in no way whatever must it affect our friendship.'

Toni felt herself relaxing as the tension left her body. She returned Aaron's smile and, reaching out, touched his hand with hers.

'You have been and are such a wonderful friend,' she said. 'I'd hate it if this came between us. And Aaron, if there is ever anything I can do to repay you for everything you have done for me, then you must promise to tell me.'

Aaron's pause was hardly noticeable before he said, 'I wonder if you really mean that? Suppose I were to say that I would consider we were well and truly back to square one if you agreed to stay on here at least until after your baby is born and stop looking at cheap little attics and basement flats in unsavoury back streets where you could get mugged.'

Toni's pause was only momentary before she returned his smile, saying: 'You sound just like my mother, Aaron.' She sighed. 'I suppose it does make sense for me to stay here if you really don't want your own privacy! But on one condition – that you allow me to pay a proper rent and some of the expenses.' When he made to protest, she added firmly: 'You said we were friends, Aaron, and friends go Dutch, don't they? I really mean it, Aaron. I've been your guest quite long enough.'

His pause was infinitesimal. Then he said, 'If that is what you want, Toni. And now that is agreed, I want to see all those brochures you are holding dumped in the waste-paper basket.' He gave her a charming smile. 'Our tenancy agreement insists on two things: that you allow me to cook the evening meal and that I allow you to have first choice of TV programme.'

'But that is all in my favour!' Toni said, smiling. 'I'll agree to you doing the cooking, but you can have first choice when it comes to the TV.'

They would be living like any married couple, she thought as she put the brochures in the wastepaper basket by her chair, at the same time worrying that all the advantages were really on her side. She would not be contributing anything other than a nominal rent and would be making herself beholden to him once more. It now crossed her mind that as Aaron seemed to lack any friends, male or female, he must be lonely. It would explain why

her companionship was so important to him that he was prepared
to offer marriage as a way of keeping her with him. The love he
had expressed for her might more properly be called need.

Later that evening, after Toni had retired to bed, Aaron sat
alone in the drawing room, his gaze no longer on the television
where together they had watched the ten o'clock news. He was
staring at the pile of brochures in the waste-paper basket. His
former feeling of victory at having gained Toni's promise to
remain living with him for a while longer had been dwarfed by
one of cold determination. She had made it quite clear to him
that her pregnancy was instrumental in her refusal to marry
him. The coming child would be a living memory of her former
lover, Justin Metcalf, who stood between him and what he wanted
more than anything in the world – what he intended to have at
any cost.

Aaron knew little about childbirth but he'd looked up the
subject on the internet and discovered that twenty-four weeks
was the limit for a legal termination. Even then he'd known
without asking that Toni would not agree to having an abortion.
Believing as he had done that it was not the child but her love
for Metcalf that stood in his way, Aaron had put his antipathy
to the forthcoming infant to the back of his mind. Now, realizing
his mistake, he also realized it would not be long before the baby
was born, and that he must be quick in devising a way to get rid
of it – a way which would not endanger himself or Toni.

Aaron stood up and walked across to the drinks bar where he
poured himself a large brandy. One stiff drink always cleared his
thinking, and he badly needed a clear head to sort out a way to
achieve his aims.

Leena's death had to some extent been opportunistic – the
condition of the snow, the absence of other skiers, her insistence
on leading the way. Now he could see no easy way to get rid of
the unborn child. The internet had implied that medication was
available which would bring about an abortion but gave no
indication of the stockist. An alternative accident such as a fall
downstairs might have the same result as Leena's accident: Toni
could be killed and, if that was not bad enough, suspicion could
fall on him.

He paced the room, the tension inside him increasing as he

faced the fact that it was not going to be easy to get rid of the unborn child – indeed, it might prove impossible. Should he therefore wait until after it had arrived when it was a separate entity and he could fabricate a cot death? If he were to play the part of a doting parent after its birth, there would be no valid reason to suspect him of causing the death.

Sitting down once more in his armchair, the colour returned to Aaron's cheeks and he came close to smiling as his imagination of the aftermath took hold. Toni would be heartbroken and he would be on hand to comfort her. She would be painfully involved with the legal consequences and he would be there to support her. It would be only a matter of time before she realized that the loss of Metcalf's child was for the best, finally closing the door on the whole unhappy affair.

Aaron's grey eyes darkened and half closed in a smile of satisfaction as he realized he had only to wait. He would make no demands upon Toni – put no kind of pressure on her to show him more affection. Instead, he would drive her down to her parents and be as charming and as caring as they could wish. He would suggest that Toni invite her former boss, Julia, to dinner one evening and ensure she saw him as the perfect replacement for the erring boyfriend. He had never found it difficult to be charming, to behave as an actor might, playing the part of the romantic lead. As for Toni herself, he need only behave with constraint – show her affection, care and understanding, but never pressurizing her into more than she felt able to give him.

It never once crossed Aaron's mind that, however carefully he planned, he might not achieve exactly what he wanted.

TWENTY-TWO

I t was nine o'clock in the morning when Justin's plane touched down at Gatwick Airport. He hurried down the long passageway to Arrivals, impatient to find a quiet corner from which he could telephone Toni. She was not answering her mobile. Perhaps she had gone back to her old job, he thought, but was informed by her tactful former boss, Julia Nilson, that Toni was probably down in Oxfordshire with her parents.

Making no further attempt to reach her on her mobile, Justin decided he would catch the Gatwick Express up to London, retrieve his car from the underground garage and drive straight down to Hook Norton, where he now assumed he could find her.

He glanced at his watch. If all went well he would be able to leave London by two o'clock and, if the traffic wasn't too bad, meet up with Toni at teatime.

By the time Justin was finally on the M40, a great deal of his renewed self-confidence had vanished. It was all very well for his mother to insist that Toni's refusals to answer his calls or see him the last time he had flown back to England was an instant reaction and one Toni was now regretting. It did not matter which of the two of them was responsible for their quarrel; if he swallowed his stupid pride and returned to England again, all might be put right between them. Now, driving as fast as he could down the motorway, he wished he could be more certain that time had softened Toni's attitude towards him; that she still loved him and he could convince her of his innocence.

Watching for the turn-off to Banbury, he began to feel even more unsure of Toni's response. Buoyed up by indignation at the unfairness of the situation and her lack of faith in him, he'd stopped trying to contact her. Why, he'd complained to his mother, should he be the one to make a second attempt to effect a reconciliation when it was Toni's refusal to give him the benefit of the doubt which had been the cause of their separation?

He recalled his parents' decision to leave Nice and sail on to

Spain and the Algarve, where there were some excellent golf courses. His father had wanted him to go with them but it was then that his mother, noting Justin's depression, had pointed out that he was letting his pride stand in his way – besides which, she'd added, both she and his father were getting tired of seeing his miserable face. That was the moment he had made up his mind to try to make a second attempt at a reconciliation. As soon as they reached the Portuguese coast, he had immediately gone ashore and booked a flight back to England from Faro Airport for the following day.

Turning left on to the familiar road to Hook Norton, Justin's anxiety increased. What would Toni's reaction be when she saw him? Should he have telephoned her mother first? Supposing Toni was not there? Supposing she refused to see him?

Pulling himself together, he drove on into the village and drew to a halt outside Cherry Tree Cottage. Parking his Alfa Romeo in front of the house, he walked up the path and rang the doorbell. Mrs Ward answered almost immediately. Her look of surprise as she recognized him quickly gave way to one of anxiety as he asked to speak to Toni.

'She isn't here, Justin!' Mrs Ward told him uneasily. Toni had told her of their quarrel and although she herself had no reason to dislike Justin, both she and her husband had thought him too young and immature to be taking on the responsibilities of marriage. They considered the kindly Aaron Osborn far more suitable, and their hopes had been raised when Toni agreed to make use of the accommodation he had offered her in his flat.

'Toni has gone back to Mr Osborn's flat in London,' she said and added tentatively, 'I can give you her mobile number if you haven't got it . . .'

'Thank you, Mrs Ward, but I do have it,' Justin replied, trying to conceal his shock at the thought of Toni back with Osborn. 'I assume his address is the same as it was before she came out to join me and my family abroad.'

Mrs Ward's nod seemed to him to come reluctantly, but he didn't mind. Disappointing as it was not to find Toni at her parents' house, he now knew where she was. He'd never really liked Aaron Osborn, and he and Toni had once come quite close to having a row about him when he'd suggested the guy's feelings were not as platonic as he tried to make out.

Refusing Mrs Ward's invitation to stay and have a cup of tea or a beer, Justin got into his car and drove slowly back to London. He wasn't hungry. His mind was buzzing with disturbing thoughts. Could Toni – his Toni – have taken up with Aaron Osborn on the rebound? Despite the unhappy episode on the yacht and Toni's impulsive departure, he'd never really accepted that their relationship was over for good. Somewhere deep inside him, he was certain they would make up the quarrel just as soon as he could convince her of his innocence. They belonged together and, but for her parents' intervention, they would have been happily married by now.

Quite suddenly, Justin's confidence deserted him as a thought struck him: what could be more likely than that Toni, believing he'd been having an affair with Marisse, should have turned to another man for comfort?

Justin had been heading for Aaron's flat in Clapham but he now braked sharply and turned back towards the centre of London. He manoeuvred his way through the traffic into Park Lane and stopped outside the Grosvenor Hotel. Giving his keys to the doorman, who was always ready to park his Alfa in the hotel's underground car park, he made his way to the bar.

As usual in the evening, it was at its busiest and Justin opted to sit on a bar stool rather than occupy one of the few empty tables. He'd barely had time to order himself a pint of lager before the man sitting on his left addressed him.

'Thought you'd moved into a flat of your own, Justin!' he said. 'Good to see you!'

Justin turned to look at the dark-haired young man on the stool beside him. His face broke into a smile.

'Didn't expect to run into you, Andy!' he said to his neighbour, who he now recognized as one of his former university friends. 'I've only just got back from abroad and I'm using the parents' suite here until I can get my flat sorted. You staying here?'

His friend shook his head. 'Only here to dine with my uncle. The old boy is doing one of his matchmaking stunts.' He grinned. 'He's the rich member of the family. Paid for my education, bless him! Never got married so I'm the one who has to carry on the

family name. Keeps finding "suitable" wives for me. Invites me
up to London to have a meal and introduces me to whoever is
new on the list of possibles.'

They both laughed.

'So who's on offer today?' Justin asked.

'Well, no one, actually! That's to say, the girl he'd had up his
sleeve is no longer in the land of the living.' He paused to grin
at Justin, and said that his elderly relative, whilst delightful in
most other ways, still lived in the age when matchmaking was
the norm for well-to-do or titled families.

'I gather he'd had his eye on a half-Indian girl, an only child
and very wealthy. So dear old Uncle Fergus, hearing she was
recently widowed, jumped in on my behalf, and telephoned to
invite her to lunch . . .' He broke off, grinning. 'Turned out it
was she who had died in a skiing accident, not her husband.
Fellow called Osman, something like that.'

Justin caught his breath. Was it possible that Andy was referring
to Toni's friend, Aaron Osborn? Or were the names just similar?

There was a slight pause whilst Andy ordered new drinks for
them both, then continued: 'Good old Uncle Fergus then got
wind of the rumour going round that because the girl was
extremely wealthy, the father suspected the husband of killing
her because he was her sole beneficiary. Nobody believed it
because the guy nearly died, too. Anyway, Uncle Fergus thought
it wasn't fair to do me out of a decent dinner, so here I am –
minus a future wealthy bride.'

'Bad luck!' Justin said. Then the smile slowly faded from his
face and, frowning, he added: 'What did you say the husband's
name was . . . is? I think I may know him.'

'Osborn. Just remembered: Aaron Osborn. Strange bloke. I
met him once.'

Justin was silent, his thoughts whirling. Osborn. Aaron Osborn
– Toni's friend, the guy in whose flat she had been living after
she had leased her own; the guy with whom she was now staying,
according to her mother; the sympathetic guy who had promised
to give Toni his messages that night he'd followed her back to
England asking her to get in touch with him . . .

'It all sounded a bit iffy,' Andy was saying as he helped himself
to a handful of salted peanuts. He laughed. 'Reckon good old

Uncle Fergus had his head screwed on – young, pretty widow and loads of dosh. Would have suited me!'

He glanced at his watch and stood up suddenly. Paying the barman, he apologized to Justin for rushing off but said he'd only just noticed it was six o'clock when he was due to meet his uncle in the lounge.

After his friend had gone, Justin stayed on at the bar lost in thought as he finished his beer. Was it really possible that Andy had been talking about Aaron Osborn and his late wife? Andy had described the accident which had killed the wife as 'a bit iffy'. Surely it was only on TV detective programmes that such things took place? He wished now that Andy had stayed longer so he could have obtained more details. The Osborn he'd talked about certainly sounded like the guy Toni had befriended in hospital in Spain, and who was now repaying her good deeds by letting her stay in his lavish apartment. Toni had described its opulence when she had stayed there before flying out to join him in France.

Thoroughly uneasy, there was a deep frown on Justin's face as he hurried out of the hotel and climbed into his car, which the doorman had fetched for him. As he crossed the Thames and headed towards Clapham his anxiety increased. If – and it was a big if – it had been Aaron Osborn who had killed his wife and got hold of her money, he would no longer need wealth but might well be wanting a pretty wife. Toni had always described their relationship as being that of really good friends, but everyone knew that it was only a small step from friendship to love. Toni might very easily have turned to Osborn on the rebound. It would explain, now he came to think about it, why she had not stayed with her parents for a while after flying back to England but rushed back to London to the comforting arms of the waiting boyfriend.

Reaching Clapham Common, Justin tried to calm his thoughts. He had begun to suspect that Osborn may not have passed on his messages to Toni that night he'd flown back from France hoping to convince her that he had not been having an affair with Marisse. That night, he had thought how unlike Toni it was not to allow him another chance to explain the situation to her. Well, this evening he would not leave Osborn's flat until he had seen her. Now there was not just his own desperate hopes for a reconciliation to be considered, but Toni's safety. However unlikely it might be, if Osborn had killed his wife . . .

His concerns were brought to an abrupt halt as he parked outside the entrance to the block of flats overlooking Clapham Common. After getting a ticket from the parking meter and locking his car, he climbed the six steps to the front door and rang the bell for Osborn's flat. He had to do so three times before a female voice answered:

'Mr Osborn is out and won't be back for an hour or so – please don't ring again.'

It was Toni's voice, recognizable although distorted by the box in front of him. Justin immediately put his finger on the bell again and left it there. When still it was not answered he went back to his car, unlocked it and, leaning inside, pressed the horn with his hand and kept it there.

A window opened high above and Toni looked down to the street below. Justin recognized her at once, even with her hair wrapped up in a white bath towel. His heartbeat quickened as memories of Toni's hair-washing sessions flashed into his mind – him coming up behind her as she bent her soapy head forward under the shower, he leaning forward to cup her naked breasts in his hands; how finally her wet hair had soaked them both because he had not given her time to dry it before making love to her. He recalled how once, before she had cut her long hair, she'd tied it round his wrists and whispered, 'Now you are my prisoner and I'll never let you go!'

Her voice carried down to him now. 'Do you want me to take a message? Or . . .' She broke off as suddenly she recognized the Alfa and knew at once who he was.

'Open the door, Toni!' Justin called back. 'I want to see *you*, not Osborn, and I'm not going away until I do.'

When still she made no move, he shouted: 'If you won't open the damn thing, I'll bash it in!'

Toni had been glancing up and down the street to see if anyone was listening, but only a speeding taxi went up the road.

'OK, I'll press the button,' she called down.

Pulling on her towelling dressing gown and fastening it tightly round her, Toni made her way into the flat's hallway. Her heart was pounding as she did as he asked, and stood listening for the sound of the lift stopping outside on the fourth floor. A few moments later, the gates of the lift clanged shut and Justin came through the open door into the flat. Toni felt a rush of mixed emotions. She had almost forgotten how good looking he was; how her body leapt to life at his physical proximity; how much she longed to be in his arms, to feel his lips on hers. Then she recalled how desperately hurtful had been his betrayal.

She moved quickly away and preceded him into the sitting room. Avoiding the black leather sofa, she sat down quickly in one of the four comfortable armchairs leaving Justin no option other than to seat himself in one of them further away. Having done so, he regarded her silently for a moment before he noticed that there was something different about her figure. She looked . . . how was it exactly? He drew in his breath sharply, his eyes narrowing in disbelief as he leaned forward in his chair and said in a quiet, uneasy tone: 'Forgive me for asking, Toni, but are you pregnant?'

Only then did Toni realize that in the emotional five minutes which had just passed, she had almost forgotten the child she was carrying – Justin's child.

'Well, are you?' he repeated. His voice was suddenly filled with bitterness as he said accusingly: 'I knew you were living with Osborn, but not . . .' He broke off, his face losing its colour as a thought came into his head. 'You were pregnant when you came to Nice, weren't you? And you had the gall to accuse *me* of being unfaithful!' His voice became too choked to continue.

Toni cried out impulsively: 'It's your baby, Justin! Yes, I was pregnant when I came to Nice, pregnant with *your* baby. I was going to tell you but then . . . then . . .' She burst into tears.

Stunned, Justin tried to absorb what Toni had just said. A baby . . . his baby . . . He felt overwhelmed by a mixture of emotions.

Slowly, he rose from his chair and crossed the room to kneel at Toni's feet. Grasping both her hands he asked huskily: 'You're having my baby?'

Toni nodded. 'There's never been anyone but you. I loved you, Justin, and that night . . . the night before you left to join your parents . . . that night was . . . well, it was special, wasn't it?'

Justin recalled it very clearly. They had been out dancing, their bodies pressed closer and closer as the evening wore on. When finally he had driven her back to his flat and they closed the front door behind them, they'd made love there in the hall, too impatient in their need for each other to wait until they were in bed; too impatient for either to worry that they had no birth control. When it was over and with arms around each other they had made their way to bed, Justin had said, 'Let's hope I haven't just given you a baby, my darling.' And Toni had replied with a loving kiss: 'More likely twins!'

Several minutes passed before Justin could find his voice. Then, holding tightly to Toni's hands, he said urgently: 'I do remember . . . how could I not? Oh, Toni, I know you don't, but please, please trust me. I swear on my life that I never had an affair with Marisse. After you left, she did finally admit she'd told you that we had, but I was still angry with you for rushing off the way you did without trusting my word. When I'd calmed down, I came back to England to tell you Marisse had been lying, but when you didn't return my phone calls—'

'What phone calls?' Toni interrupted. 'What are you talking about?'

Justin caught his breath. 'You weren't answering your mobile so I rang Osborn. He said you were out and he'd ask you to ring me back when you returned.'

Toni's face whitened in distress as she said quickly: 'He never gave me the message, Justin.' Before he could speak, she added tentatively, 'Maybe he forgot—'

She broke off as Justin, his eyes stormy and his voice harsh, said, 'I should have guessed it. I just assumed you didn't want to talk to me. That man's a bastard! He's in love with you. One thing I'm sure of is that you aren't safe here with him.' He stood up and looked down at her, before adding sharply: 'You're not in love with him, are you?'

Toni shook her head. 'No, of course not. I love you, Justin. I've never stopped loving you. But I'm not just going to walk out on Aaron without warning. He's been a wonderful friend to me, and I trust him absolutely. He's been very, very kind to me and he doesn't have many friends and . . .'

'Then give him a week's notice!' Justin said urgently. 'Toni, don't you see we can be married now. With the baby coming, your parents will be all for it. I love you so much, more than I can begin to tell you. I want to take care of you. If you weren't happy living with me, then after the baby is born, I wouldn't stand in the way of a divorce if that was what you wanted. I just want you to be happy.'

Neither he nor Toni had heard the front door of the flat being opened by Aaron, who had returned from a visit to his tailor. He stood now in the doorway of the sitting room staring from one to the other, a strange enigmatic look in his eyes, his jaw rigid.

Justin got to his feet and moved awkwardly back to his chair as Aaron said coldly: 'It's you, Metcalf, isn't it?' His voice now turning icy, he turned to look at Toni.

'I thought you had made up your mind to exclude this un-savoury character from your life, Toni? Do you want me to throw him out for you?'

Despite the extra weight she was carrying and with disregard for any harm which could be done to her baby, Toni was quickly on her feet and standing between the two men. Before either could speak, she said quietly: 'Please stop this right now! Justin, please go. I promise I will get in touch with you. Aaron, we need to talk. I would have told you if I had known Justin was coming to see me. I hadn't arranged to see him when I knew you would be out.' She turned back to Justin.

'Please go, Justin!' she repeated. 'You have my word I will phone you.'

For one long minute, Justin stood where he was, staring at Toni's white, anxious face. Although he was sorely tempted to stay, he concluded that it might be better not to confront Osborn at this moment. If the guy believed Toni was going to leave him, there was no telling how he would react. Justin was no longer in any doubt that the man was in love with Toni. No doubt he was doing everything he could to indicate what a good husband he would make – seemingly a good father for the baby, too. Well, it wasn't his baby and Toni wasn't his. There was something about the man that he didn't trust: something he could not put a name to but which he sensed was threatening – not to Toni, perhaps, but certainly to him.

For the immediate present, Justin thought, Toni was in no danger, and he could wait a bit longer for her to move back in with him.

Nevertheless, he now decided, he would not leave without

telling Toni again how much he loved her. Disregarding Aaron's presence, he stepped forward and took Toni's hand and pressed it to his lips. He saw the colour flood into Toni's cheeks, and she repeated softly that she would ring him. Then, turning away, he was aware of nothing else but the threatening glare in Aaron's steely grey eyes, and the ominous expression on his face as he opened the front door to see him out.

It was at that moment as he stood staring unseeingly at the closed door that Aaron realized his hope of ultimately turning Toni's love from her former boyfriend to himself had vanished. That hope had magnified ever since she had returned from France swearing she never wanted to see Metcalf again. She had made it clear to Aaron that she liked him, considered him a wonderful friend upon whom she could depend – someone she could turn to whenever she was in trouble. Her parents did not try to hide their approval, and he had been clever enough to disguise his antipathy when she'd told him about the baby.

His mouth twisted in sudden anger. Fate might be doing its best to thwart him but he would not be deterred from trying to claim Toni for himself. It would not be difficult if they were married for him to get rid of the baby. It was Metcalf who stood in his way. But how to get rid of him? It would be almost impossible if they were known to be enemies. He must contradict all the unpleasant things he had said to Toni about the man – make out he had been over-cautionary on her behalf.

Such thoughts churning through his mind, he walked back into the sitting room. Seemingly without further hesitation, his voice softening, he said, 'I'm sorry, Toni, really sorry! I had no right whatever to speak of Metcalf in such derogatory terms. I'd made up my mind to hate him because he was making you so unhappy. It's obvious to me now that the scheming French girl was the cause of the upset. Your poor guy must have been devastated when you upped and came back to England.'

'Oh, Aaron!' Toni exclaimed. 'You don't know how happy that makes me to hear you admit you misjudged Justin. I did, too, didn't I?' She smiled happily. 'You are my very best friend and I'd absolutely hate it if you and Justin didn't like each other so we can all meet up in the future. Now . . . well, I couldn't be happier. You're a star!'

Aaron managed a thin smile. 'Tell you what,' he said, 'why don't the three of us have a drink together? I suggest you stay the night, do your packing, and when he comes to collect you tomorrow we'll have a farewell drink!'

Toni shook her head. 'No, not a farewell, Aaron. We're going to see lots of each other, I promise.' She was very tired and needed to sleep. One more night without Justin was disappointing but not a hardship, she told herself, and Aaron's plan for the three of them to have a friendly drink the next morning before she left was a good one.

'My mobile is by my bed,' she continued. 'I'll go and ring Justin now and tell him what we've planned.'

Feeling as if a weight had been taken off her shoulders, Toni went to her bedroom. The flat was so well centrally heated that she did not bother to close the door when she sat down on the edge of the bed to make the promised phone call to Justin. She wasn't sure how he would receive her request that he should accept Aaron's apology and stay for a drink the next day, but he was so relieved and happy to know she was going back to him that he agreed reluctantly to Aaron's plan.

'You don't have to be best friends, darling,' Toni reassured him. 'He really *has* been a wonderful friend to me – which reminds me, could you possibly bring a bottle of Hardys viognier with you, his favourite, which I can give him as a sort of thank you for letting me use his flat . . .'

In the doorway of the sitting room, Aaron stood silently listening, thinking bitterly that a bottle of wine would hardly compensate for the fact that Toni was about to leave him. The thought was intolerable, and he went back into the sitting room and poured himself a stiff whisky.

There was a bottle of perfectly good viognier in his fridge, he thought wryly. What he'd like to do in the morning was tell Metcalf to get out of his house and take his wretched bottle with him . . .

Aaron's thoughts came to an abrupt halt and his heart started thumping furiously as a solution to his problems suddenly filled his mind.

TWENTY-THREE

Aaron's hand was shaking with excitement as he dialled the combination on the door of the small safe in his wardrobe. Opening the door, he reached behind a velvet-covered box containing all Leena's priceless diamond and gold jewellery, and drew out a small phial. Holding it up to the light, he breathed a sigh of relief. The contents had not solidified or changed colour in any way. Closing the safe, he carried the small phial through to the kitchen.

His heartbeat quickened as he took his own bottle of Hardys viognier out of the fridge and, placing it on the kitchen table, he opened it carefully and poured in the contents of the phial. He then closed the bottle with the same meticulous care. He took it through to the sitting room where he placed it out of sight on the drinks bar. Satisfied that it would not be seen by Toni or Metcalf when they came into the room, he walked across to his usual place beside the window and drew back the curtains.

Outside it was teeming with rain and an angry wind was bending the tops of the trees on the Common. It was a depressing sight but Aaron was unmoved by it as he recalled the fortuitous occasion when he had come by the lethal poison now in his bottle of wine.

He had bought it from a fellow patient in the hospital who had lost both legs and an arm. He'd said it was a lethal dose which would 'put you out of your misery once and for all' if he reached the point of thinking life wasn't worth living. Somehow the guy had managed to hide it from the hospital staff.

Aaron now recalled how deeply depressed he had been at the time when the amputee had wheeled himself through to his ward at a nurse's request to 'cheer him up'. The guy had refused to tell him where he had got hold of the poison but said he no longer wanted it; that he'd bought it for a very large sum of money, but since then had become a Roman Catholic and his new religion barred all forms of suicide. It had not stopped him from selling the stuff to him and, with Leena's wealth safely in his bank account, he could afford to buy it.

At that time, he had himself been close to suicidal, but the unexpected offer of a visit from Toni had put such thoughts out of his mind. He had then decided to keep the stuff in case he ever had a use for it in the future. It was almost, he now thought, as if Fate had decreed the time would come when he wanted to get rid of the man who stood between him and the only person in the world he had ever truly loved.

Returning to the kitchen to prepare a breakfast tray for Toni, he went over in his mind how clever was his plan to kill Metcalf without the need to dispose of his body – it would be taken to the morgue for a post-mortem. Toni would be in a state of shock and he would be there to console and support her. The coming baby would be a temporary inconvenience but he had already chosen a convenient cot death after a month or two during which he would appear devoted to the child. There was also the possibility that the shock of Metcalf's sudden death might bring on a miscarriage – a preferable solution but not one he could control.

He glanced at his watch again and saw that it was after eight o'clock and time to take Toni's breakfast tray in to her. It was one of the small ways he spoiled her, and he knew he would be rewarded with her lovely smile when she thanked him.

After Aaron had left the room, and she had finished her breakfast, Toni relaxed against her pillows, a feeling of relief replacing the anxiety which had disturbed her night's sleep. By the sound of Aaron's voice when he had brought in her tray, and his carefree expression, she was able to reassure herself that he was not after all as depressed by her coming departure as she had expected. Justin had promised to be friendly, so unless he reneged on his word she and Aaron could remain friends in the future. As she put aside her tray and got out of bed, she found herself wondering if perhaps he had decided he would finally carry out his proposal to join a gym, start swimming again, and get some real strength back into his muscles. Whatever it proved to be, it was a huge relief to her to see him so cheerful. He had proved such a wonderful, caring friend, doing everything he possibly could to make her happy. And now, despite the fact that he was in love with her, he was befriending Justin just to please her. He was, without doubt, the most selfless person she knew.

After having a quick shower, she put on the new black Top Shop maternity trousers she had bought when her baby bump had made her jeans and skirts impossible to wear, and over them a loose jumper. Then, making up her face and tying back her hair, she packed all her remaining belongings into her suitcase and zipped it up. Glancing round the room, she made certain she had not left anything behind before she went to join Aaron in the sitting room. He was polishing glasses behind the bar. Seeing her, he put down the teacloth and joined her on the sofa.

'You're looking very pretty, Toni,' he said. 'That's a new way you have done your hair, isn't it? It suits you.'

'Justin likes it swept back, too,' she replied. Noticing the almost imperceptible tightening of Aaron's mouth, she realized at once that it had been tactless to have pointed out that she was hoping for Justin's approval rather than his.

'Only ten o'clock!' he remarked. 'Two hours to go before your guy arrives. Want to watch telly? Or shall we have a game of chess? I shall miss the games we've had.' He placed a hand lightly on hers, adding: 'You've become quite a good player, Toni. Were we to have had a few more battles, I think you might well have won one or two!'

Relaxing, Toni smiled, knowing that Aaron was only flattering her. He was a very skilled player, foreseeing the result of every move. It was part of his nature, she thought as she helped him set out the chessmen: the very opposite of Justin and herself, who both acted impulsively without thought of the consequences.

She and Aaron were absorbed in their third game when at a quarter to twelve, Justin rang the bell. Getting to her feet, Toni said, 'I'll let him in,' and hurried into the hall to open the door. A few minutes later, the lift gate opened and Justin stood there, looking a trifle sheepish. Handing her a bag in which was a bottle of wine, he said, 'I know you said twelve, hon, but I couldn't wait to see you.' He reached out and put his arm round her, drawing her against him and kissing her hungrily. 'You look so good!' he whispered. 'Oh, Toni, darling, say you've missed me! Say you love me! I can't wait to get you back to the flat. Do we *have* to stay for a drink?'

She hugged him, a smile of purest happiness on her face. 'Yes, we do, darling. Just for an hour! I do so want you and Aaron to be friends. He's terribly sorry he was so rude to you yesterday. Promise me you'll be nice to him!'

Justin's handsome face was distorted momentarily by a grimace. 'As it's to please you, I promise. But don't expect me to kiss him,' he joked.

Laughing, Toni tucked her arm through his and led him into the sitting room. A faint smile curved Aaron's mouth as he crossed the room and held out his hand.

'Good of you to come!' he said, his voice friendly. Before Justin could reply, Toni stepped between them and handed Aaron the bag Justin had given her containing the bottle of wine. Feigning surprise, Aaron drew out the bottle exclaiming: 'Hardys viognier! Absolutely my favourite! What's more, I'm right out of it at the moment.' He looked at Justin. 'I suspect Toni told you it was on my shopping list?'

'Yes, I did,' Toni said quickly. 'It's just a small contribution to today's little celebration of our future friendship.' She took a step forward and, reaching up, kissed Aaron's cheek.

With a huge effort, Aaron forced a smile as he nodded at Justin and carried the bottle across to the bar. 'Good of you to bring it!' he said to Justin. 'Sit yourselves down, both of you, and I'll open this bottle. Feels cold enough to me, and I for one will infinitely prefer it to the Jacob's Creek I've got in the fridge.'

Justin and Toni sat down on the sofa, holding hands. Seeing them, Aaron's mouth tightened imperceptibly as a surge of jealous rage swept through him. Unable to waste a moment's time, he placed Justin's bottle behind the bar and quickly retrieved his own. Holding it up, he said, 'Hope you like this wine as much as I do!'

Justin grinned, saying: 'To be truthful, I like pretty well anything! My father is always telling me I should educate my palate.'

Forcing a smile, Aaron put the two glasses and tumbler he had prepared on top of the bar. Filling the tumbler first from a carton of orange juice for Toni, he poured out a glass of wine from his bottle and took them both across to the coffee table in front of the sofa. Returning to the bar, he lifted Justin's bottle of wine, which he had already opened, and poured out wine for himself.

Holding up the bottle, he said to Justin: 'Don't know what you think, but I think we should chill it down a bit more. I'll get the ice bucket. Won't be a minute. Don't wait for me!'

Exchanging the bottles once again, he left the bar, carried the polluted bottle into the kitchen and poured the contents down the sink. A quick glance into the sitting room revealed a scene exactly resembling his plan – Metcalf with his glass of wine in one hand, Toni holding her tumbler of juice, her lovely face turned up to his with an adoring expression. The cold, biting stab of jealousy he felt at the sight caused his hand to shake, but, seconds later, a smile returned to his lips. *Let her give her love, her heart, to someone else: someone who had only minutes to live,* he told himself. *Soon, very soon, I'll be holding her weeping, beautiful body in my arms.*

Reaching for the tray of ice cubes in the freezer, he looked up sharply as he heard the sound of breaking glass and the thud of a body as it hit the floor. Smiling, he put down the ice cubes and hurried to the door, blissfully unaware that he would see Toni and not Justin Metcalf crumple in a heap on the sitting-room floor.

TWENTY-FOUR

I t was yet another freezing cold winter's day and Aaron tucked his hands deeper into his anorak pockets. Risking the loss of power in his car battery, he put on the heater for a further five minutes. His eyes never once left Justin's Alfa Romeo, which was also in the hospital car park nearby. It was the fourth day of his secret vigil, Justin having only left the hospital for an hour each morning, presumably to go home and change his clothes.

For the umpteenth time, Aaron's mind returned to the dreadful mistake he had made. It was said that every murderer makes one mistake . . . he had made two.

He should not have given Justin his glass of wine and left the room. His second mistake was overlooking the fact that Toni knew he kept half-a-dozen bottles of his favourite wine under the shelf in the larder. Now, when the poison had been detected, Toni could tell them that by no means was Justin's bottle of wine the only one in his flat, thus proving that he could have poisoned a wine bottle himself and substituted it for Justin's.

Twenty-four hours had passed before he had realized with a terrible sense of shock that he had no alternative but to kill Toni if she survived the poisoning, the only person in the world he had ever loved. An investigation would reveal the question mark over the circumstances of Leena's death and Mr and Mrs Ward could testify to his possessive devotion to Toni. It would be a reason for him to attempt to kill Justin.

Justin had telephoned to tell him that Toni was now known to have been poisoned and the police had been called in to begin an investigation. Aaron had put the receiver down, too shaken to be able to reply. He knew now that it was over. He had already disposed of the wine in the larder but if he was to save his own life he had to silence Toni. He must find his passport; get money from his bank; book a passage to . . . to somewhere where he would not be found – to Japan; he spoke the language fluently and Nani would advise him where he could live and make a new life for himself.

He looked at his watch. It was nearly two o'clock; a time when convalescent patients rested before their visitors arrived and the nurses and doctors were not constantly in and out of the rooms. He counted on their absence now. As he got out of his car and walked towards the big front doors, he thought with surprising detachment what must now be done if he was to survive.

His thoughts of the future ceased as he saw a number of people coming out of the main door and walking towards their cars. He waited behind a car lest Justin was among them, and suddenly saw him some distance behind the group. He was glancing at his watch before moving away to where his car was parked. Aaron waited a few minutes and then hurried across the wet tarmac and in through the big doors. With no way of knowing for how long Justin would be gone, he was aware of the need for speed. He hurried across the hall to the reception desk and enquired where he might find Toni. He was sent up to the Primary Care floor where he was told by a nurse that Antonia Ward was not allowed visitors.

Aaron smiled disarmingly. 'Yes, I know!' he said. 'But I'm her brother. I have been abroad and have only just got back to England and been told my sister was dangerously ill. She must have been wondering why I did not visit her sooner. If it's OK with you, I'll just pop in for a minute or two and tell her I'll be back tomorrow.'

As a safeguard, he had disguised himself sufficiently to be unrecognizable, with dark-rimmed glasses, a fashionable four-day stubble, and he had replaced his usual smart trousers and jacket with jeans and an old anorak.

'It was an awful shock hearing Toni was so ill!' he continued. 'I was on holiday in South Africa when I got the text from her boyfriend telling me it was touch and go. I can't tell you what a relief it was when I got back yesterday to hear she was out of intensive care.'

The nurse regarded him sympathetically. 'Your sister is still very ill,' she said. 'You may find her a little tearful – she lost her baby, you see.'

Aaron nodded. 'Yes, her boyfriend told me. Well, I'll just pop in to give her a hug and let her know I'm back home again.'

The nurse pointed to an open door a little further down the corridor. Unhurriedly, Aaron walked down to it and went inside, closing the door softly behind him.

Toni was sleeping. Her lashes were dark against the extreme pallor of her cheeks. It seemed to him that her face had narrowed, her cheeks hollowed. There were tubes everywhere attached to drips, drains, an oxygen cylinder, and a wire with a bell on the end hung over one shoulder. For a moment, shock held him immobile. Then he moved towards the bed. In a soft, almost hypnotic tone, he said, 'There was a time when you loved me, I know there was . . . When I was in Stoke Mandeville and you came to visit me. You were different from my wife . . . you cared. Leena never cared the way you did – all she wanted was for me to make love to her and when I couldn't . . .' His voice hardened. 'She deserved to die.'

He broke off once more, his tone now becoming almost childish as he muttered: 'You loved me, I know you did. We could have been happy, Toni, I know we could. I would have taken such care of you and you would have loved me if Metcalf . . . He should have died. But he's not going to have you, Toni. I couldn't stand it day in and day out knowing you were loving him instead of me . . .'

His voice trailed into silence and he moved to the side of her bed. Toni was breathing softly, her lips slightly parted. Above her head was a spare pillow and he reached up to take it.

'I'm sorry! I'm so sorry,' he murmured. At that moment, the door opened and the nurse he had spoken to earlier came in. The colour drained from Aaron's face and, catching his breath, he said quietly, 'I thought she might be more comfortable with an extra pillow!' Then, forcing himself to move unhurriedly, he smiled at the startled nurse and walked out of the door.

EPILOGUE

Toni lay on a sun lounger overlooking the bigger of the two Hotel Los Palmeros swimming pools. Her eyes were closed so she did not see the woman approaching her.

'Toni! It is Toni, isn't it?'

Toni opened her eyes and leaned up on one elbow. 'Gemma!' she exclaimed. 'What a lovely surprise! Justin and I weren't sure if you and Peter were out here this spring. We've just arrived!'

The older woman sat down on the end of the lounger and, readjusting her sunglasses, she replied: 'We came the day before yesterday. We didn't hear from you at Christmas, so we wondered if you'd decided to holiday somewhere else. Your last holiday here ended somewhat disastrously in hospital, didn't it?'

Toni nodded. 'I'm sorry there was no Christmas card, Gemma, especially as you were so good to me those last few days.' She paused briefly before adding: 'I was in hospital for quite some time over Christmas. One thing after another went wrong before that and . . . well, cards weren't on our agenda. I'm just so happy you and Peter are out here, too. Justin will be thrilled to have a golf partner. I can't play at the moment because . . .'

She broke off, determined not to let the threatening tears fall. Then pulling herself together, she said, 'I had a miscarriage. I was rather ill and I lost my baby. It was a little girl.' She gave a weak smile as she added quickly: 'Don't say you're sorry or I shall start crying.'

Gemma quickly bit back the sympathetic words she had been about to speak and said gently: 'I understand, my dear. Several years ago I had two miscarriages myself. Then Peter and I decided to give up trying for a baby. We decided we were perfectly happy just with each other.' She squeezed Toni's hand and added: 'You're looking very thin and pale but I'm sure this lovely Spanish sunshine and the luscious hotel food will soon put the colour back into your cheeks.'

For the first time since she had come out of hospital, Toni felt able to talk about the ordeal of the last five months. Her parents had been too horrified, too shocked, for her to burden them with details, but this warm-hearted, friendly woman was someone she trusted and in whom she felt she could confide.

'It was over four months ago that I was rushed into hospital,' she said. 'They thought I was going to die. I thought so, too,' she added with a weak smile.

Gemma's kind face was filled with concern, but she kept her voice casual as she replied: 'How absolutely rotten for you! Poor old Justin must have been beside himself with worry. Men being the way they are, I imagine the fear of losing you far outweighed any sadness at losing the baby.'

Toni nodded. 'Justin and I don't talk about it. He said I mustn't think about it, and when I am really well again, we'll try for another baby if that's what I want.'

When Toni had started confiding in Gemma, she had only intended to tell her about the miscarriage, but now suddenly she wanted desperately to confide the whole horrific story to which there was, at present, no conclusion. In a low, husky voice, she said, 'Do you remember, Gemma, that invalid I sort of befriended in Carlos Haya hospital last spring? The man whose wife had been killed falling down a mountain?'

Gemma nodded. 'Indeed I do! He was paralysed if I remember rightly, after falling himself when he tried to rescue her.'

Toni nodded. 'I visited him in hospital in England and we became friends, close friends, and he put me up in his flat when I was waiting to fly out to join Justin and his parents on a world cruise. I hadn't been able to go with him as I couldn't leave my job.'

Gemma nodded. 'I recall you writing about the cruise in the last letter we had from you.'

Toni's expression was wistful as she said, 'I won't go into it, but when I did join him, we had a rather nasty quarrel and I came home. I was pregnant at the time but I hadn't yet told Justin as I was so angry with him. Anyway, I'd let my flat to a friend, so Aaron, the paralysed man who, by the way, had made a quite miraculous recovery, let me stay in his spare room.'

She paused to draw a deep sigh before saying: 'I know it was naïve of me but I didn't realize he was in love with me, so I stayed on there until Justin flew home wanting to make up our quarrel, and of course I was desperate to make up, too.'

Gemma smiled. 'Peter and I always said you were the most loving couple we'd ever met!'

It was Toni's turn to smile, but only briefly. 'Everything was fine again and Justin was coming round to Aaron's flat in the morning, staying for a quick drink before taking me home with him. That's when it happened . . .' She broke off, struggling not to cry.

Gemma took her hand and held it tightly. 'My dear girl, you don't have to talk about it if it upsets you.'

'But I do want to!' Toni said huskily, brushing away the threatening tears. The words now poured from her. 'We were to have this farewell drink. I was only drinking orange juice – because of the baby. Aaron had gone to the kitchen to get an ice bucket and Justin wanted me to take a sip of his wine so we could sort of toast each other, and I did. I don't remember much after that – only the agonizing pain and Justin holding me in the back of Aaron's car as he drove us to St Thomas's hospital, begging me not to die.'

Her voice trembled and she paused briefly. 'Aaron brought the bottle of wine with us in case that had made me ill and I might need an antidote. Justin said Aaron was as terrified as he was because he thought that I was going to die. I hadn't eaten or drunk anything since breakfast so Aaron said he thought it must have been the wine Justin had bought on his way from the off-licence when he was coming to collect me.'

'So it *was* the wine?' Gemma gasped, looking horrified.

Toni nodded. 'When the police were told that the poison – I don't recall the name – had indeed been detected in Justin's bottle, he was arrested because he couldn't deny it was his. At the time I was too ill to know Justin had been detained in a cell overnight. He was released next day after being questioned but had his passport taken away and was forbidden to leave the country.'

'How awful for him!' Gemma exclaimed.

Toni grimaced. 'I was in intensive care, what with the poisoning and the inevitable miscarriage, so I couldn't do anything to help him. He told me later that Aaron, too, had been taken in for

questioning and that was when they called both his and Justin's
names up on their computer database. Justin wasn't on it, of
course, as the most he'd ever been done for was speeding.'

She gave a weak smile before continuing in a distressed tone.
'Aaron immediately became their number-one suspect because
they had his wife's death on record. Apparently her father had
lodged a formal accusation in England when the Spanish authorities declared her death had been accidental.'

Gemma was disbelieving as she said, 'But you told me how
sympathetic and caring the man had been and that he was in
love with you.'

Toni nodded. 'That was the very reason they decided he
must somehow have put poison in the wine: that he wanted to
dispose of Justin so I would be free to marry him. Justin had no
motive for killing Aaron because I was able to tell them I was
on the point of leaving Aaron's flat to go back with Justin and
we planned to get married.'

Gemma now did her best not to look too horrified by Toni's
story. It must have been unbelievably awful for her and small
wonder that she lost the baby.

'I'm so sorry, my dear! Thankfully you can now put all that
in the past.'

Toni shook her head. 'Not quite!' she said. 'You see, Aaron
disappeared. When he knew he was on the point of being arrested,
he just vanished. For three weeks, we heard nothing more and
then we were told by the police that they had traced his flights
by various routes to Japan, where he was born. Then, a few
weeks after that, they discovered that he had been to Kobe where
he visited his old Japanese nanny and borrowed some yen from
her. Then he just disappeared. Since then, nobody has been able
to find out where he went. There's no doubt Aaron wanted to
kill Justin,' she continued in a shaky voice. 'Justin insists he is
a mental case – it's almost certain he killed his wife, you know.
So he could inherit her money.'

It was several minutes before Gemma could find her voice, so
shocked was she by Toni's story. Seeing her expression, Toni
reached out and put her arm round Gemma's shoulder.

'Don't look so horrified!' she said with a faint smile. 'Justin
thinks I'm crazy because in many ways I'm glad Aaron is lost:

that he can't be tried for attempted murder when everything would have come out about my quarrel with Justin and me living in Aaron's flat and everything.' She paused briefly before adding: 'Nobody will ever know for sure what happened on that mountain in Spain, although Justin says that it's obvious Aaron wanted his wife's money – then, having got it, he wanted me.' She gave a wry smile. 'If Justin had his way, he said he'd have him hung, drawn and quartered.'

'And I quite agree with him, Toni!' Gemma said sharply. 'Just because the man was kind to you doesn't alter the fact that he would have killed your beloved if you hadn't tasted Justin's wine before he did. For heaven's sake, you might have died. What I don't understand is how, if he somehow managed to put poison in Justin's bottle, he was going to avoid drinking it himself.'

Toni sighed. 'Justin thinks he must have had another bottle of viognier – Aaron usually kept one or two although he swore he was out of wine that day – and had intended giving us champagne but preferred the viognier. I don't suppose we'll ever know. I used to have nightmares in hospital but only occasionally now.

'Justin and I have agreed not to talk about it any more. He wants Aaron imprisoned for life. I suppose it is pathetic of me but I half hope they never find him. Justin gets angry when I say that, so I never talk about it.'

She smiled suddenly and held out her hand. 'My wedding ring!' she said. 'We got married three weeks ago in Hook Norton where my parents live. Justin's family flew home for it. They wanted us to have our honeymoon on the yacht but Justin and I decided to come back here. The last time we stayed, we were just pretending to be married!'

Before Gemma, who was smiling now, could offer her congratulations, a waiter passed them carrying a tray of empty glasses. She beckoned him over and ordered two Pimms, which arrived very promptly with a bowl of delicious Spanish black and green olives and plates of nuts and crisps.

'How's Peter?' Toni asked once they had raised their glasses to each other. 'Justin will be so pleased to find a golf partner,' she repeated. 'He went up to Golf das Aguilas hoping they would be able to get him one. If Peter's on his own . . .'

'He is!' Gemma broke in. 'He'll be over the moon now your

Justin is here. I broke my wrist at Christmas so my poor dear husband hasn't got his favourite partner – me – and that's because he knows he'll always win our matches. He hates losing!' she added, laughing.

'Justin's just the same!' Toni said. 'I hope they stay friends. Justin is in the process of buying a golf course in partnership with one of his old school chums, a guy called Matt, and he says when they start up they'll need all the friends they have to come and play there, until they have enough members to become an economical entity'

'How exciting!' Gemma said. 'And how brave of them in this recession. Is it in Spain?'

Toni shook her head. 'No, in Oxfordshire, which is good because I won't be too far from my parents. My father had a stroke last summer. He has recovered but he's quite frail, so my mother will be happy to have me nearby. I'm so pleased for Justin, Gemma,' she added. 'Ever since he left school he worked for his father and he's been wanting for ages to find a job he really enjoyed and for which he was qualified.'

'His own golf course!' Gemma exclaimed. 'Peter will be hugely interested!'

Toni smiled. 'I'm so happy for Justin!' she said again. 'It's like he's won the lottery! When we go home, he's off to Ashridge for a management course so he'll know about the business side of it once the building is finished and it's ready for the off. They've bought a nine-hole course, you see, and enough unwanted land adjacent to it to turn it into eighteen holes eventually. Justin's parents and Matt's are putting up the capital.'

'I can't wait to tell Peter all this!' Gemma said.

'If he has partnered Justin, then he will already have heard more than enough about it,' Toni said, laughing. 'That's all he talks about!'

They were still enjoying their drinks when the two men appeared together. Both had played to their handicaps and were in excellent spirits. All four now agreed to meet for coffee in the cocktail bar later that evening.

Half an hour later, Toni and Justin were alone in their suite. Justin had bribed Alfonso in reception to put them in the same room as they'd had on their previous visit. They were now able to sit on their spacious south-facing balcony overlooking the bright blue Mediterranean Sea beyond the garden. Gradually the sky became tinged with pink as the sun began to sink. The house martins were sweeping down to the pool, dipping their beaks in the water before soaring up above into their nests in the crevices of the hotel walls. Directly below in the garden, the pool area was slowly becoming deserted by the hotel guests who were moving back in groups to the hotel to prepare for the evening.

Justin placed a glass of iced water on the chair beside Toni and poured himself a glass of San Miguel beer from a bottle in the fridge. Sitting down beside her, he took her hand in his, saying: 'I don't think there is anywhere in the whole world I'd rather be and certainly not with anyone but you. I love you, Toni, so much!'

Toni drew a long sigh. 'I love you too, Justin. It frightens me sometimes when I think how easily things can go wrong. I so nearly lost you.'

Justin shook his head. 'Another time we will both know better than to mistrust each other. Trust is so very important in a relationship, isn't it?' After a minute, he added: 'My God, Toni, when I think how nearly we lost each other!'

His eyes were thoughtful and his hand tightened around hers. 'Clever place for Osborn to hide out, Japan! If they do eventually manage to trace him there, I wonder if the Japs will extradite him. We may not have an agreement with Japan. Could be months, years before he can be tried in England, if ever. Look at that train robber, Ronald Biggs. He only came back because he was dying.'

'We have agreed not to think about Aaron,' Toni reminded him. 'The last thing we want is three people on our honeymoon!'

Justin drew her to her feet and hugged her, saying huskily, 'I love you, Toni. I love you so much! Did that punctilious doctor of yours say he would allow me to make love to you?'

Toni smiled. 'As it so happens, I did ask him. I told him we had just got married and were about to go on our honeymoon.'

Justin gave a quizzical smile. 'So what did the old dragon say?'

'You know perfectly well, Justin, that he's not an old dragon: he was always very kind to me. You're just jealous because I like him so much.'

Justin snorted. 'All right, so I'm jealous, but what I want to know is, what did he say?'

Toni stifled a giggle. 'He said intercourse would do no harm provided it was not too turbulent.'

'Turbulent! Hells bells!' Justin said indignantly. 'What did he think I might do?' Then his scowl gave way to a grin. 'OK, so I get the message.'

Toni smiled. 'If you'd like to risk it now . . .'

She got no further before Justin was leading her back into the bedroom and over to their king-sized bed.

Three hours later, they sat holding hands in the cocktail bar as they waited for Peter and Gemma to join them. In front of them on the table was a bottle of champagne – courtesy of the hotel. There were two other couples and three families in the room, and in one corner, a four-piece orchestra was playing a Spanish song. When it ended, it was followed by another.

'Remember this, darling?' Justin said, turning to Toni. 'I think it's "*Solo por Tu*".'

Toni grinned as Justin's arm tightened around her shoulders. 'As if I could forget that sexy female – name of Carmellia del Concordia, if I'm not mistaken. She could have eaten you alive!'

Justin laughed. 'Well, you can't blame me for enjoying her come-on!' he said. 'She was quite something!' His expression suddenly became serious. 'But you should have trusted me, my darling! I was in love with you. I'd never have been unfaithful to you – not with Carmellia or with that wretched French girl, Marisse. You've got to learn to trust me!'

Toni nodded. 'And you've got to learn to trust *me*. You thought I was half in love with Aaron, didn't you?'

Without waiting for an answer, her eyes swimming with tears, she said suddenly: 'Our baby, Justin. They said I must teach myself to look forward, not back . . .' She paused briefly while she regained her composure. 'We'll have another baby, won't we? Not now . . . not yet, but in a year or two, won't we?'

Justin squeezed her hand once more. 'We won't just have one, we'll have two, three, four if that's what you want, my darling.'

He broke off as at that moment, the vocalist, a good-looking young Spaniard with large, soulful brown eyes, slowly crossed the room to their table. With barely a glance at Justin, he stood with his eyes searching Toni's face and asked if she had any special request she would like them to play for her.

'What about "Spanish Eyes"?' Toni suggested as she returned the young man's smile.

'*Si, señora*,' he said and, with another admiring glance, returned to his fellow players.

Justin's forehead was creased in an unmistakeable frown as he said, 'For heaven's sake, he's got a cheek singling you out like that! Were you smiling at him and made him think . . .?'

Toni lifted her hand and with two fingers touched his lips, saying: 'He is quite a dish but no, I wasn't flirting with him. Now who's not trusting again?'

Justin's scowl vanished instantly and was replaced by a smile. 'OK! So you love me and I trust you even if you were flirting with the guy,' he said softly. 'All the same, my darling, don't ever forget . . . you are my wife now and you belong to me!'

'That's right,' Toni said, adding with a twinkle in her eye, '*Solo por tu, Señor!*'

They were both laughing happily as Peter and Gemma arrived.